The Sea Is My Brother

JACK KEROUAC

The Sea Is My Brother

Introduction by Dawn Ward

DA CAPO PRESS
A Member of the Perseus Books Group

Typeset in 12 point Dante by Cynthia Young at Sagecraft.

Cataloging-in-Publication data for this book is available from the
Library of Congress.

First Da Capo Press edition 2012
Reprinted by arrangement with Penguin Classics, an imprint of Penguin Books
ISBN: 978-0-306-82125-7
E-Book ISBN: 978-0-306-82128-8

Published by Da Capo Press
A Member of the Perseus Books Group
www.dacapopress.com

Da Capo Press books are available at special discounts for bulk purchases
in the U.S. by corporations, institutions, and other organizations. For more
information, please contact the Special Markets Department at the Perseus
Books Group, 2300 Chestnut Street, Suite 200, Philadelphia, PA 19103, or call
(800) 810-4145, ext. 5000, or e-mail special.markets@perseusbooks.com.

10 9 8 7 6 5 4 3 2 1

Introduction

The first major work by Jack Kerouac, *The Sea Is My Brother* was written in the spring of 1943 and until now has never been published in its entirety. The novel offers the reader a glimpse of a Jack who is at odds with his own youthful idealism and the harsh realities of a nation at war. His character studies reveal much of what we expect from Jack's observational style providing many glimpses into his early writing experiments while presenting us with an introspective view of Jack as a young man played out in the two main characters. Everhart who is encouraged by his new friend, the reckless and high-spirited Martin, to hitchhike to Boston and sign up as a Merchant Marine, finds himself taking risks that he never would have considered before meeting Martin. This contradiction, embodied in the two main characters, Bill Everhart and Wesley Martin, is exemplified in their first meeting: "Everhart studied the stranger; once, when Wesley glanced at Everhart and found him ogling from behind the fantastic spectacles, their eyes locked in combat, Wesley's cool and non-committal, Everhart's a searching challenge, the look of the brazen skeptic."

Jack began several stories based on his adventures at sea with different titles and characters. He did make a few starts on the first chapter of this story as well which contains some enlightening notes by Jack concerning the development of the novel's characters around what he felt was his own dual personality.

> Soon, I knew I was too old to persist in my boyhood ways. Reluctantly, I gave it up. (Someday, I'll explain to you the details of this world—they are enormous in number and complex to a point of maturity.)
>
> Thus on the one side, the solitary boy brooding over his "rich inner life"; and on the other, the neighborhood champ shooting pool down at the club. I'm convinced I shouldn't have picked up both these personalities had I not been an immense success in the two divergent personality-worlds. It is a rare enough occurrence . . . and none of the Prometheans* seem to have these two temperaments, save, perhaps, [George] Constantinides.

---

*A group of Jack's friends from Lowell which included: Sebastian Sampas, Cornelius Murphy, George Constantinides, Billy Chandler, George Apostolos, John MacDonald, Ed Tully and Jim O'Dea who met informally to discuss various topics including literature and the arts.

Naturally enough, my worldly side will wink at the wenches, blow foam off a tankard, and fight at the drop of a chip. My schzoid self, on another occasion, will sneer, slink away, and brood in some dark place.

I've gone to all this trouble, outlining my dual personality, for a purpose besides egocentricity. In my novel, you see, Everhart is my schzoid self, Martin the other; the two combined run the parallel gamut of my experience. And in both cases, the schzoid will recommend Prometheanisms (if I may coin the phrase), and the other self (Wesley Martin) will act as the agent of stimulus—And as in all my other works, "The Sea Is My Brother" will Assert the presence of beauty in life, beauty, drama, and meaning. . . .

The majority of Everhart's character is derived from Jack's own experiences. Everhart's intellectual pursuits, for example, can be achieved with very little risk, for he lives with his father, brother, and sister much like Jack. Everhart's desire to experience something more real and stimulating, echoes Jack's recent rebellious voyage on the *Dorchester* and his dropping out of Columbia. Therefore Everhart's decision to take a leap-of-faith symbolizes in many ways Jack's desire to turn away momentarily from his intellectual self and use his perceptive nature to inspire his work. Jack noted this need for real experiences in his journal: "My mother is very worried over my having joined the Merchant Marine, but I need money for college, I need adventure, of a sort (the real adventure of rotting wharves and seagulls, winey waters and ships, ports, cities, and faces & voices); and I want to study more of the earth, not out of books, but from direct experience" (July 20, 1942).

The character Martin on the other hand is free of any intellectual burdens; this is Jack's "worldly side," is free to come and go with no strings attached. A wanderer of the world, Martin goes from port to port taking in the experiences without fear or commitment. In a letter to Jack's friend Sebastian Sampas in November 1942, he tries to convince him to ship out with him in the Merchant Marines: "But I believe that I want to go back to sea . . . for the money, for the leisure and study, for the heart-rending romance, and for the pith of the moment." Jack's notes on another working copy of the novel reinforce his intention to include every aspect of his worldly experience: "Into this book, 'The Sea Is My Brother', I shall weave all the passion and glory of living, its restlessness and peace, its fever and ennui, its mornings, noons and nights of desire, frustration, fear, triumph, and death. . . ."

In the same letter to Sebastian Jack laid out the internal soul-searching dilemma that *The Sea Is My Brother* is attempting to resolve:

I am wasting my money and my health here at Columbia . . .

I am wasting my money and my health here at Columbia . . . it's been one huge debauchery. I hear of American and Russian victories, and I insist on celebrating. In other words, I am more interested in the pith of our great times than in dissecting "Romeo and Juliet" . . . . at the present, understand. . . . Don't you want to travel to the Mediterranean ports, perhaps Algiers, to Morocco, Fez, the Persian Gulf, Calcutta, Alexandria, perhaps the old ports of Spain; and Belfast, Glasgow, Manchester, Sidney, New Zealand; and Rio and Trinidad and Barbados and the Cape; and Panama and Honolulu and the far-flung Polynesians . . . I don't want to go alone this time. I want my friend with me . . . my mad poet brother.

The references about wasting money at Columbia parallel Everhart's internal questioning "What was he doing with his life?" and become his impetus for shipping out with Martin. Amongst Jack and his friends from Lowell there was much correspondence during this time. They wrote of comrades and brotherhood, topics which are an integral part of this novel and help to resolve Jack's battle with his changing political views. When he was younger his infatuation with the idealism expressed in the letters to his friends and the ongoing dialogs in the media regarding the various political movements give way to his more critical nature which began to develop after his induction into the Navy. He wrote to Sebastian on March 25,1943 from the Navy barracks: "Though I am skeptical about the administration of the Progressive movement, I shall withhold all judgments until I come in direct contact with these people—other Communists, Russians, politicians, etc., leftists artists, leaders, workers, and so forth."

The Sea Is My Brother is a seminal work marking Jack's transition as a writer and represents the earliest evidence of the development of his style. He tells Sebastian in a letter, dated March 15, 1943; "I am writing 14 hours a day, 7 days a week . . . I know you'll like it, Sam; it has compassion, it has a certain something that will appeal to you (brotherhood, perhaps)."

Shortly after he wrote *The Sea Is My Brother,* Jack began *The Town and the City*, published in 1950, which launched his career as a writer. These two novels, both based on his real-life experiences, are part of the writing method he started to develop in 1943 that he dubbed "Supreme Reality."

Jack began this work not long after his first tour as a Merchant Marine on the *S.S. Dorchester* from the late summer—October of 1942 during which he kept a journal detailing the gritty daily routine of life at sea. The journal titled "Voyage to Greenland" is dated 1942 and subtitled "GROWING PAINS or A MONUMENT TO ADOLESCENCE". Inspired by the trip, the journal is an example of

Jack's love for adventure, the character traits of his fellow shipmates which created spontaneous sketches of those experiences that were later woven into this novel.

Jack often revisited his journals adding notes and did so here with a poem dated April 17, 1949 several years after the *Sea Is My Brother* was written.

> All life is but a skull-bone and
> A rack of ribs through which
> we keep passing food & fuel—
> just so's we can burn so
> furious beautiful.

The first entry dated Saturday July 18, 1942 describes his first night on deck the *Dorchester*, the meal he ate (five lamb chops), and this passage written early the next morning: "I sat in a deck chair, awhile after and bethought me about several things. How should I write this journal? Where is this ship bound for, and when? What is the destiny of this great grey tub? I signed on Friday, or yesterday, and do not begin work till Monday morning. . . . I could have gone home to say goodbye—but goodbyes are so difficult, so heart-rending. I haven't the courage, or perhaps the hardness, to withstand the tremendous pathos of this life. I love life's casual beauty—fear its awful strength."

Early on in the "Voyage to Greenland" journal is evidence of his plans for the observations he was making: "Up to now, I've refrained from introducing any characters in this journal, for fear I should be mistaken due to a brief acquaintance with those in question, and should be forced to rescind previous opinions and judgments." Jack continues that although it would create an "acceptable log," that he felt it should "tell the story within the story," and that since he shall "perhaps one day want to write a novel about the voyage," and he would be able to find all the details on file: "a true writer never forgets character studies, and never will." Later the same day he began these character studies.

August 2
CHARACTER STUDIES

Here is some data on my scullion mates, and others: Eatherton is just a good-hearted kid from the "tough" section of Charleston, Mass, who tries to live up to his environment, but fails, for his smile is too boyish, too puckish. He is a veteran seaman already, and berates me for being a despicable "college man" who "reads books all the time and knows nothing about life itself." Don Graves is an older boy, quite handsome, with a remarkable sense of wit and tomfoolery that often befuddles me. He is able to toy with people's emotions, for he undeniably possesses a strong, moving personality. He's 27 years old, and I believe he looks upon me with some mixed pity and head-shaking—but no compassion. He has little of that, and no learning; but considerable earthy judgment and native ability, and a sort of appeal that is quiet and sure. Eddie Moutrie is a cussing little bastard, full of venom and dark, haggard beauty, often tenderness. I envision him now, smoking with his contemptuous scowl, turned away, yelling derision at me in a rough, harsh voice, returning his gaze with blank and tender eyes.

August 2
MORE

They are good kids, but cannot understand me, and are thus enraged, bitter, and full of hidden wonder. Then there is the chef, a fat colored man with prominent buttoxes [sic] who loves to play democratic and often peels potatoes with us. His face is fat and sinuous, touched with childish propriety. His face seems to say: "Now, we are here, and things are in all due harmony and order." He has grown fat on his own foods. He sits at our mess table, wearing a fantastic cook's cap, and picks delicately with fat greasy hands at his food. All things are in order with the chef. He is the antithesis of Voltaire, the child of Leibniz.

Then there's Glory, the giant negro cook, whose deep voice can always be heard in its moaning softness above the din of the galley. He is a man among men—gentle, impenetrable, yet a leader. The glory that is Glory . . .

"Shorty" is a withered, skinny little man without teeth and a little witch jaw. He weighs about 90 pounds, and when he's mad, he threatens to throw us all through the portholes.

"Hazy" is a powerfully built, ruddy

August 2
LES MISERABLES

Youth who works, eats, and sleeps, and rarely speaks. He's always in his bunk, sleeping, smiling when Eatherton farts toward his face: then turns over back to his solitary, sleepy world.

"Duke" Ford is a haggard youth who has been torpedoed off Cape Hatteras, and who carries the shrapnel marks of the blast in his neck. He is a congenial sort but the frenzied mark of tragedy still lingers in his eyes; and I doubt whether he'll ever forget the 72 hours on the life raft, and the fellow with bloody stumps at his shoulders who jumped off the raft in a fit of madness and committed suicide in the Carolinian sea . . .

Then there's the rather stupid Paul, an awkward, almost idiotic youth, the butt of all the leg-pullers in the crew. They are making a mess of the tenderness his mother must have taught him. His voice is a strange mixture of kindness, despair, and futile attempts at snarling pseudo-virility. It is pathetic to see this poor lad in the midst of callous fools and stupid bums . . . for most of the crew is just that, and I shall not write of them except

August 2
VAL, THE LADIES' CHOICE

as a man body in this narrative. They have no manners, no scruples, and spend their leisure time gambling in the dining room, their dull countenances glowing with ancient cruelty under the golden lights. O Satan! Mephisto! Judas! O Benaiah! O evil eyes that glint beneath the lights! O clink of silver! O darkness, O death, O hell! Sheathed knives and chained wallets: lustful, grabbing, cheating, killing, hating, laughing in the lights . . .

Jack's journal ends on August 19, 1942 shortly after reaching Greenland. The last entries are a short story entitled "'WHAT PRICE SEDUCTION?' OR A 5 CENT ROMANCE IN ONE REEL A SHORT SHORT STORY— 'THE COMMUNIST,'" two poems, a descriptive character piece called "PAT," and a set of notes called JACK KEROUAC FREE VERSE, FOUR PARTS.*

This next poem encompasses many of the daily frustrations expressed in the journal about being different than the rest of the crew.

---

*These journals and notes can be found in the Jack Kerouac archive, Berg Collection at the New York Public library.

WHEN I WAS OUT TO SEA

Once, when I was out to sea,
I knew a lad who's famous now.
His name is sung in America,
And carried far to other lands.
But when I knew him, far back now,
He was a lad with lonely eyes.
The bos'un laughed when Laddie wrote:
"Truth Brothers!" in his diary.
"You daggone little pansy!"
Roared the heavyset rough bos'un.
"You don't know what life be,
You with all your sissy books!
Look at me! I'm rough and I'm tough,
And I got lots to teach ye!"
So the bos'un jeered, and the bos'un snarled,
And he set him down to drudgery.
And the boy, he and his poetry,
He wanted to stand bow-watch
And brood into the sea,
But the bos'un laughed, and snarled,
And set him down to drudgery.
Down in the hold, mid fetidity . . .
Then one night, a wild dark night,
The lad stood by the heaving bow
And the storm beat all about him.
The bos'un he laughed and set right out
To put him down to drudgery,
That sissy lad of poetry . . .
With wind and sky all scattered wide,
A grim, dreary night for fratricide!

–JK

Jack disembarked the *Dorchester* but continued to think of the sea as a symbol for the integration of his friends and the promise of brotherhood. After a brief return to Columbia University he moved back to Lowell with his parents and got a job at a garage on Middlesex Street where he works diligently night and day writing by hand his first novel. The novel's importance to this early period of Jack's life is indisputable. Although a short novel, it represents a pivotal point in his writing career where his serious intention to become a writer resonates in the power of his speech and the depth of his visualization.

The placement of hyphens, dashes, ellipses, apostrophes, etcetera, have all been maintained only standardized for readability. In cases of spelling errors, I have corrected unless thought to be intentional and have included some editorial elements and or additional punctuation when needed which can be found in brackets [. . .] and in cases were material is missing, illegible or otherwise obscured, I have shown this with empty brackets [ ]. In places where Jack Kerouac has edited his own material by crossing out and re-writing; I have only included that which he preserved unless context is unclear or words appear to be missing. Spacing and line breaks have been preserved in some cases where the emphasis of the words would be affected, otherwise the margins, indents and line spacing have been standardized. Kerouac's entire archive can be found in the Berg Collection of the New York Public Library.

CHAPTER ONE

The Broken Bottle

A young man, cigarette in mouth and hands in trousers' pockets, descended a short flight of brick steps leading to the foyer of an uptown Broadway hotel and turned in the direction of Riverside Drive, sauntering in a curious, slow shuffle.

It was dusk. The warm July streets, veiled in a mist of sultriness which obscured the sharp outlines of Broadway, swarmed with a pageant of strollers, colorful fruit stands, buses, taxis, shiny automobiles, Kosher shops, movie marquees, and all the innumerable phenomena that make up the brilliant carnival spirit of a midsummer thoroughfare in New York City.

The young man, clad casually in a white shirt without tie, a worn gabardine green coat, black trousers, and moccasin shoes, paused in front of a fruit stand and made a survey of the wares. In his thin hand he beheld what was left of his money—two quarters, a dime, and a nickel. He purchased an apple and moved along, munching meditatively. He had spent it all in two weeks; when would he ever learn to be more prudent! Eight hundred dollars in fifteen days—how? where? and why?

When he threw the apple core away, he still felt the need to satisfy his senses with some [   ] dawdle or other, so he entered a cigar store and bought himself a cigar. He did not light it until he had seated himself on a bench on the Drive facing the Hudson River.

It was cool along the river. Behind him, the energetic thrum of New York City sighed and pulsed as though Manhattan Island itself were an unharmonious wire plucked by the hand of some brazen and busy demon. The young man turned and swept his dark, curious eyes along the high rooftops of the city, and down toward the harbor where the island's chain of lights curved in a mighty arc, sultry beads in the midsummer mist strung in confused succession.

His cigar held the bitter taste he had wanted in his mouth; it felt full and ample between his teeth. On the river, he could distinguish faintly the hulls of the anchored merchant ships. A small launch, invisible except for its lights, glided a weaving path alongside the dark freighters and tankers. With quiet astonishment he leaned forward and watched the floating points of light move slowly downriver in liquid grace, his almost morbid curiosity fascinated by what might have seemed commonplace to another.

This young man, however, was no ordinary person. He presented a fairly normal appearance, just above average height, thin, with a hollow countenance notable for its prominence of chin and upper lip muscles, and expressive mouth lined delicately yet abundantly from its corners to the thin nose, and a pair of level, sympathetic eyes. But his demeanor was a strange one. He was accustomed to hold his head high, so that whatever he observed received a downward scrutiny, an averted mien that possessed a lofty and inscrutable curiosity.

In this manner, he smoked his cigar and watched the Drive saunterers pass by, for all outward purposes at peace with the world. But he was broke and he knew it; by tomorrow he would be penniless. With a shade of a smile, which he accomplished by raising a corner of his mouth, he tried to recall how he had spent his eight hundred dollars.

The night before, he knew, had cost him his last hundred and fifty dollars. Drunk for two consecutive weeks, he had finally achieved sobriety in a cheap hotel in Harlem; from there, he recalled, he had taken a cab to a small restaurant on Lenox Avenue where they served

nothing but spare ribs. It was there he'd met that cute little colored girl who belonged to the Young Communists
League. He remembered they'd taken a taxi down to
Greenwich Village where she wanted to see a certain
movie. . . . wasn't it *Citizen Kane?* And then, in a bar on
MacDougall Street, he lost track of her when he met up
with six sailors who were broke; they were from a destroyer in dry-dock. From then on, he could remember
riding in a taxi with them and singing all kinds of songs
and getting off at Kelly's Stables on 52nd Street and going
in to hear Roy Eldridge and Billie Holliday. One of the
sailors, a husky dark-haired pharmacist's mate, talked all
the time about Roy Eldridge's trumpet and why he was
ten years ahead of any other jazz musician except perhaps
two others who jammed Mondays at Minton's in Harlem,
Lester somebody and Ben Webster; and how Roy Eldridge
was really a phenomenal thinker with infinite musical
ideas. Then they had all rode to the Stork Club, where another sailor had always wanted to go, but they were all too
plastered to be admitted in, so they went to a dime-a-
dance joint where he had bought up a roll of tickets for
the gang. From there they had gone to a place in the East
Side where the Madame sold them three quarts of Scotch,
but when they were finished, the Madame refused to let

them all sleep there and kicked them out. They were sick of the place and the girls anyway, so they rode uptown and west to a Broadway hotel where he paid for a double suite of rooms and they finished the Scotch and flopped off in chairs, on the floor, and on the beds. And then, late the next afternoon he woke up and found three of the sailors sprawled about in a litter of empty bottles, sailor caps, glasses, shoes, and clothing. The other three had wandered off somewhere, perhaps in search of a bromo seltzer or tomato juice.

Then he had dressed up slowly, after taking a leisurely shower, and strolled off, leaving the key at the desk and making a request to the hotelkeeper not to disturb his slumbering buddies.

So here he sat, broke except for fifty cents. Last night had cost $150 or so, what with taxis, drinks around, hotel bills, women, cover charges, and everything else; his good time was over for this time. He smiled as he remembered how funny it was when he woke up a few hours previous, on the floor between a sailor and an empty quart bottle, and with one of his moccasins on his left foot and the other on the bathroom floor.

Casting away his cigar butt, he rose and moved on across the Drive. Back on Broadway he walked slowly uptown taking in the small shoe stores, radio repair shops, drugstores, newsstands, and dimly lit bookstores with a calm and curious eye.

In front of a fruit stand he stopped in his tracks; at his feet, a small cat mewed up at him in a plaintive little cry, its pink bud of a mouth opened in a heart shape. The young man stooped down and picked up the cat. It was a cute little kitten with grey-striped fur and a remarkably bushy tail for its age.

"Hello, Tiger," he greeted, cupping the little face in his hand. "Where do you live, huh?"

The kitten mewed a reply, its fragile little frame purring in his hand like a delicate instrument. He caressed the tiny head with his forefinger. It was a minute shell of a skull, one that could be crushed between thumb and forefinger. He placed the tip of his nose against the little mouth until the kitty playfully bit it.

"Ha ha! A little tiger!" he smiled.

The proprietor of the fruit stand stood in front rearranging his display.

"This is your cat?" inquired the young man, walking over with the kitten.

The fruit man turned a swarthy face.

"Yes, that is my wife's cat."

"He was on the sidewalk," said the young stranger. "The street's no place for a kitty, he'll get run over."

The fruit man smiled: "You are right; he must have wandered away from the house." The man glanced up above the fruit store and shouted: "Bella!"

A woman presently came to the window and thrust her head out: "Hah?"

"Here's your cat. He almost got lost," shouted the man.

"Poom-poom!" cooed the woman, espying the kitten in the young man's hands. "Bring it up Charley; he'll get hurt in the street."

The man smiled and took the cat from the stranger's hands; its weak little claws were reluctant to change hands.

"Thank you!" sang the woman from above.

The young man waved his hand.

"You know women," confided the fruitseller, "they love little cats . . . they always love the helpless things. But when it comes to men, you know, they'll want them cruel."

The young stranger smiled thinly.

"Am I right?" laughed the man, slapping the youth on the back and reentering his store with the kitten, chuckling to himself.

"Maybe so," mumbled the youth to himself. "How the hell should I know?"

He walked five more blocks uptown, more or less aimlessly, until he reached a combination bar and cafeteria, just off the Columbia University campus. He walked in through the revolving doors and occupied an empty stool at the bar.

The room was crowded with drinkers, its murky atmosphere feverish with smoke, music, voices, and general restlessness known to frequenters of bars on summer nights. The young man almost decided to leave, until he caught sight of a cold glass of beer the bartender was just then setting before another patron. So he ordered himself a glass. The youth exchanges stares with a girl named Polly, who sits in a booth with her own friends.

They stared at each other for several seconds in the manner just described; then, with a casual familiarity, the young man spoke to Polly: "Where *you* going?"

"Where am I going?" laughed Polly, "I'm not going anywhere!"

But while she laughed at the stranger's unusual query, she could not help but wonder at his instant possessiveness: for a second, he seemed to be an old friend she had forgotten many years ago, and who had now chanced upon her and resumed his intimacy with her as though time were no factor in his mind. But she was certain she had never met him. Thus, she stared at him with some astonishment and waited for his next move.

He did nothing; he merely turned back to his beer and drank a meditative draught. Polly, bewildered by this illogical behavior, sat for a few minutes watching him. He apparently was satisfied with just one thing, asking her where *she* was going. Who did he think he was? . . . it was certainly none of *his* business. And yet, why had he treated her as though he had always known her, and as though he had always possessed her?

With an annoyed frown, Polly left the booth and went to the young stranger's side. She did not reply to the inquiries shouted after her by her friends; instead, she spoke to the young man with the curiosity of a child.

"Who are you?" she asked.

"Wesley."

"Wesley what?"

"Wesley Martin."

"Did I ever know you?"

"Not that I know of," he answered calmly.

"Then," began Polly, "why did you? . . . why? . . . how do you . . . ?"

"How do I do what?" smiled Wesley Martin, raising a corner of his mouth.

"Oh hell!" cried Polly, stamping an impatient foot. "Who *are* you?"

Wesley maintained his amused shadow of a smile: "I told you who I was."

"That's not what I mean! Look, why did you ask me where I was going? That's what I want to know."

"Well?"

"Well for God's sake don't be so exasperating—I'm asking you, you're not asking me!" By this time Polly was fairly shouting in his face; this amused Wesley, for he was now staring at her wide-eyed, with his mouth open, in a fixed, sustained glee which was all at once as mirthless as it was tremendously delighted. It seemed as though he were about to burst into guffaws of laughter, but he never did; he only stared at her with roguish stupefaction.

At a point where Polly was ready to be hurt by this uncomplimentary attitude, Wesley squeezed her arm warmly and returned to his beer.

"Where are you from?" pressed Polly.

"Vermont," mumbled Wesley, his attention fixed on the bartender's operations at the tap.

"What're you doing in New York?"

"I'm on the beach," was the reply.

"What's that mean?" persisted Polly in her child's wonder.

"What's your name?" posed Wesley, ignoring her question.

"Polly Anderson."

"Polly Anderson—Pretty Polly," added Wesley.

"What a line!" smirked the girl.

"What's that mean?" smiled Wesley.

"Don't give me that stuff . . . you all try to act so innocent it's pitiful," commented Polly. "You mean men don't have lines in Vermont? Don't try to kid me, I've been there."

Wesley had no comment to make; he searched in his pockets and drew out his last quarter.

"Want a beer?" he offered Polly.

"Sure—let's drink them at my table; come on over and join the party."

Wesley purchased the beers and carried them over to the booth, where Polly was directing a new seating arrangement. When they had seated themselves side by side, Polly introduced her new friend briefly as "Wes."

"What do you do, feller?" inquired the man addressed as Everhart, who sat in the corner peering slyly through horn-rimmed glasses toward Wesley.

Wesley glanced briefly at his interrogator and shrugged. This silence fascinated Everhart; for the next few minutes, while the party regained its chatty frolic,

Everhart studied the stranger; once, when Wesley glanced at Everhart and found him ogling from behind the fantastic spectacles, their eyes locked in combat, Wesley's cool and non-committal, Everhart's a searching challenge, the look of the brazen skeptic.

As the night now wore on, the girls and George Day in particular became exceedingly boisterous; George, whose strange fancy had thought of something, was now laughing with a painful grimace; he was trying to relate the object of his mirth, but when he would reach the funny part of the incident which amused him so, and was about to impart the humor to the rest of them, he would suddenly convulse in laughter. The result was infectious: the girls screamed, Everhart chuckled, and Polly, head on Wesley's shoulder, found herself unable to stop giggling.

Wesley for his part, found George's dilemma as amusing as he had Polly's impatience earlier in the evening, so that now he stared with open-mouthed, wide-eyed astonishment at the former, an expression of amusement as droll in itself as anything its wearer would ever wish to see.

For the most part, Wesley was not drunk: he had by now consumed five glasses of beer, and since joining the party in the booth, five small glasses of straight gin which Everhart had cheerfully offered to pay for. But the atmosphere of the bar, its heavy smoke and odor of assorted hard liquors and beer, its rattle of sounds, and the constant loud beat of music from the nickelodeon served to cloud his senses, to hammer them into muffled submission with a slow, delirious, exotic rhythm. Enough of this, and Wesley was as good as drunk; he usually could drink much more. Slowly, he began to feel a tingle in his limbs, and he found his head swaying occasionally from side to side. Polly's head began to weigh heavily on his shoulder. Wesley, as was his wont when drunk, or at least almost drunk, began to hold a silence as stubborn as the imperturbability which accompanied it. Thus, while Everhart spoke, Wesley listened, but chose to do so in strict, unresponsive silence.

Everhart, now quite intoxicated, could do nothing but talk; and talk he did, though his audience seemed more concerned with maintaining the ridiculous gravity of drunkards. No one was listening, unless it was Wesley in his oblique manner; one of the girls had fallen asleep.

"What do I tell them when they want to know what I want to do in life?" intoned Everhart, addressing them all with profound sincerity. "I tell them only what I won't do; as for the other thing, I do not know, so I do not say."

Everhart finished his drink hastily and went on: "My knowledge of life is negative only: I know what's wrong, but I don't know what's good . . . don't misinterpret me, fellows and girls . . . I'm not saying there is no good. You see, good means perfection to me . . ."

"Shut up, Everhart," interposed George drunkenly.

". . . and evil, or wrong, means imperfection. My world is imperfect, there is no perfection in it, and thus no real good. And so I measure things in the light of their imperfection, or wrong; on that basis, I can say what is not good, but I refuse to dawdle about what is supposed good. . . ."

Polly yawned loudly; Wesley lit up another cigarette.

"I'm not a happy man," confessed Everhart, "but I know what I'm doing. I know what I know when it comes to John Donne and the Bard; I can tell my classes what they mean. I would go so far as to say I understand Shakespeare thoroughly—he, like myself, was aware of more imperfection than is generally suspected. We agree on Othello, who, but for his native gullibility and naiveté, would find in Iago a harmless little termite's spite, as weak and impotent as it is inconsequential. And Romeo, with his fanciful impatience! And Hamlet! Imperfection, imperfection! There *is* no good; there is no basis for good, and no basis for moral. . . ."

"Stop grating in my ear!" interrupted George, "I'm not one of your stupid students."

"Blah!" added one of the girls.

"Yes!" sang Everhart. "A high hope for a low heaven! Shakespeare said that in *Love's Labour's Lost*! Ay! There it is! A low heaven, and high-hoped men . . . but fellows and girls, I can't complain: I have a good post in the University, as we are fond to call it; and I live happily with my aged father and impetuous young brother in a comfortable apartment; I eat regularly, I sleep well; I drink enough beer; I read books and attend innumerable cultural affairs; and I know a few women. . . ."

"Is that so!" cried George, leaning his head to sleep through the monologue.

"But that is all beside the point," decided Everhart. "The revolution of the proletariat is the only thing today, and if it isn't, then it is something allied with it—Socialism, international anti-Fascism. Revolt has always been with us, but we now find it *in force*. The writing of this war's peace will be full of fireworks . . . there are two definitions for postwar peace: The good peace and the sensible peace. The sensible peace, as we all know, is the business man's peace; but of *course* the business man wants a sensible peace based on the traditions of America—he's a business man, he's in business! This the radicals overlook: they forget the business man depends as much on business as the radicals depend on private support . . . take each away from each and the two classes disappear as classes. The business man wants to exist too—but naturally he's prone to exist at the expense of others, and so the radicals are not blind to wrong. What I want to know is, if the radicals do *not* approve of economic liberalism, or laissez-faire, or private enterprise. . . ."

"Or what you will!" added George.

"Yes . . . if so, what do the radicals approve of? Plenty, of course: I respect their cognizance of wrong, but I fail to see the good they visualize; perfect states, as is the case with the younger and whackier radicals. But the older ones, with their quiet talk about a country where a man can do his work and benefit from this work; where he can also exist in cooperative security rather than in competitive hysteria—these older radicals are a bit more discerning, but I still doubt if they know what's good: they only know what's wrong, like me. Their dreams are beautiful, but insufficient, improbable, and most of all short of the mark."

"Why is that so?" Everhart asked himself. "It is so because the progressive movement makes no provision for the spirit: it's strictly a materialistic movement, it is limited. True, a world of economic equality and cooperative cheer might foster greater things for the spirit—resurgences in culture, Renaissances—but, in the main, it's a materialistic doctrine, and a shortsighted one. It is not as visionary as the Marxists believe. I say, spiritual movements for the spirit! And yet, fellow and gentlewomen, who can deny Socialism? Who can stand up and call Socialism an evil, when in the furthest reaches of one's conscience, one *knows* it is morally true? But is it a Good? No! It is only a rejection, shall we say, of the no-Good . . . and until it proves otherwise, in the mill of time, I will not embrace it fervently, I will only sympathize with it. I must search on . . ."

"Search on!" cried George, waving his arm dramatically.

"And in the process, I shall be free: if the process denies me freedom, I will not search on. I shall be free at all times, at all costs: the spirit flourishes only in the free."

"Time marches on!" suggested Polly wearily.

"Do you know something?" posed Everhart.

"Yes I do!" announced George.

"The socialists will fight for freedom, win and write the peace—in this war or the next, and they will die having lived for the inviolable rights of man. And then will come the Humanists, when the way will have been paved for them, and these Humanists—great scientists, thinkers, organizers of knowledge, teachers, leaders . . . in short, builders, fixers, developers . . . shall lay down the foundations, in the days of no-war, for the future world of never-war. The Humanists will work and pave the way for the final and fabulous race of men, who will come on the earth in an era which the world has been bleeding toward for centuries, the era of universal peace and culture. This final, fabulous, and inevitable race of men will have nothing to do but practice culture, lounge around in creative contemplation, eat, make love, travel, converse, sleep, dream, and urinate into plastic toilets. In brief, the Great Romanticists will have arrived in full force, free to fulfill *all* of the functions of humanity, with no other worry in the world except that Englishmen still prefer Shakespeare while the world reads Everhart!"

George looked up briefly from his position under the table, where he had gone in search of an errant dime: "Why Bill, why didn't you tell me you were going to be a writer."

Bill Everhart waved an nonchalant palm: "After all this, don't you think I'd make a splendid writer?"

George made a wry face: "Stick to teaching. I think you'd make a smelly writer. Besides, Everhart, you're a hopeless pedagogue, and academic pain in the neck, and an officious little odious pedant."

"In short, Bill," added Polly with a dry smile, "you're a louse."

"And a bull-slinger to boot," said George. "A little knick-knack pouting on the shelf of time," snuffing down his nose with obvious relish, "and a nub on the face of things."

Polly began to giggle again, her long white neck craned downward revealing the fragile crucifix chain she wore. Wesley gazed at her affectionately, and placing his hand about the back of her neck, he turned her face toward his and kissed the surprised, parted lips. He found them instantly responsive and frankly passionate. Polly laughed and buried her face in his lapel, her bobbed hair a lavish brown pillow for his leaning cheek.

"Day, I still think you're a scullion," accused Everhart.

"Oh for gossakes stop this crazy talk! I'm tired. Let's go!" This was spoken by Eve, the girl who had fallen asleep. She turned to her companion, yawning: "Aren't you tired, Ginger?"

Ginger, who had maintained a bored silence most of the night, except to occasionally exchange kisses with her escort, Everhart, now yawned an affirmative reply.

"Hell no! We were supposed to get stinking drunk tonight," objected Polly from Wesley's shoulder. "We haven't done any drinking!"

"Well, let them get a bottle . . . I want to get out of this place, we've been here long enough," said Eve, removing a small mirror from her purse . . . "Oh heck, I look fiendish!"

"You haven't said much tonight, feller," said Ginger, smiling toward Wesley teasingly. She was rewarded with a thin, curving smile.

"Isn't he cute!" cried Polly, delighted.

Wesley lifted his hand playfully, as if to strike her.

"Where do you want to go now?" asked George of Eve.

"Oh let's go up. We can play the portable and dance. Besides, I've got a pair of rayons to wash for tomorrow morning."

"I thought you washed them this afternoon!" said Ginger.

"I started to read a True Story Magazine and forgot all about them."

"Dopey!"

"Let's be frolicsome!" suggested Everhart, slapping the table. "I want to get blind loaded."

"You are already, shortypants," said Ginger. "Eve, will you wash my silk stockings while you're at it . . . I need them for tomorrow night."

"I will if you pick up my toaster at Macy's tomorrow."

"Oh but I have to model tomorrow afternoon from two till four," protested Ginger, turning full body toward the other. They both reflected for a few moments while George Day yawned. "But you can pick it up after!" cried Eve.

Ginger pondered for a moment.

"It's only five blocks downtown from your place," supplied Polly, growing interested in the affairs of her world.

"But I have to get my permanent, Polly," affirmed Ginger with a trace of desperation.

"You will still have time."

"Sure!" chimed in Polly.

Ginger was trapped, and she knew it; she was trapped by the insistent logic of woman-kind, as surely as she had trapped others in her moments.

"Oh all right, I guess I can," she concluded reluctantly. The other two girls leaned back, satisfied.

Wesley, who had been watching and listening, while the other two men were in reverie, now also leaned back in satisfaction. He gazed at Polly and wondered about her: she had been behaving unusually well all night, to his thinking, but now she had betrayed her colors. Polly was a woman! But when he squeezed her arm, and Polly touched her lips to his chin, quietly saying "Boo!" and tweaking his nose, he decided women had their virtues.

"Where and when do we go?" spoke George.

"To the place," said Eve, picking up her handbag with long shiny fingers. "One of you two get a quart."

"I'll get it," mumbled Everhart. "By God, I'll get two quarts."

"Let's go," cried Polly.

In the cool night street, Polly hung from Wesley's arm and shuffled a dance step while Everhart crossed Broadway to a liquor store. The others chatted and laughed; all admitted their insobriety to one another, except Wesley, who shrugged uncertainly; they laughed.

On the way to Eve's and Ginger's, they were all very gay and marched down the side street linked six abreast while Everhart sang the Marseilleise. Near an alley, Day stopped the whole group and pledged their health with one of the quarts. They all followed suit, Wesley taking at one lift of the bottle what sure must have been a half pint of the whisky.

"You from Tennessee?" drawled Ginger while the others giggled in amazement.

"Hell no, woman!" answered Wesley with a sheepish grin.

They laughed raucously and proceeded on down the street. From then on, Wesley was aware of only three things: that he drank two more enormous draughts from the bottle; that he was in New York at night, because they were walking in a steep canyon between tall corniced buildings that leaned crazily, and the stars were very far away from all this, nodding, aloof, cool up there overhead, and sternly sober; and finally, that he discovered he was holding an empty quart bottle as they climbed the stoop to the apartment, so he turned around and hurled it far up the empty street, and when the glass shattered and the girls screamed, he wanted to tell them that was what he thought of all the talk they had made tonight.

CHAPTER TWO

New Morning

When Wesley woke up, he wasn't surprised that he didn't know where he was. He sat on the edge of the bed and was annoyed because he could see all of his clothes except the socks. After having put on his shirt, trousers, and coat he squatted on the floor barefooted and peered under the bed. His socks were not there.

He left the bedroom, glancing briefly at the sleeping Polly on his bed, and roamed through the apartment searching for his socks. He went into the bathroom, with its steamy smell of soap, and rummaged around in a welter of silk underthings, hanging rayon stockings, and castoff slips. They were not to be found; as a last resort, he peeked under the bathtub. Not there.

He rubbed his teeth with his forefinger, threw water on his face, sneezed two or three times, and shuffled off into the parlor carrying his moccasins.

Everhart was sitting by the window reading a Reader's Digest.

"Where the hell are my socks?" Wesley wanted to know.

"Oh hello Wes! How do you feel?" greeted Bill, adjusting his glasses to peer at Wesley.

Wesley sat down and put on his moccasins over his bare feet.

"Lousy," he admitted.

"I feel likewise . . . how about a bromo? I made myself one in the pantry."

"Thanks."

They went into the pantry where a fragile blue-pink light streamed in from the morning street. Everhart prepared the sedative while Wesley inspected the contents of the refrigerator, picking himself out a cold orange.

"We're the only ones up," chatted Everhart. "George sleeps late all the time. Eve left for work this morning . . . I can't say as I envy her after what she drank last night."

"Eve your girl?" inquired Wesley.

Everhart handed him the bromo: "I was with her last night; George was with Ginger."

Wesley drank down the sedative.

"Eve works at Heilbroner's, she gets off at noon. Ginger'll have to get up soon herself—she's a model. Boy! What a night . . ."

Everhart followed Wesley back into the parlor.

"Is Polly awake yet?" Bill asked.

Wesley shrugged: "Wasn't when I got up."

"You certainly are the boy with the women," laughed Everhart, turning on the radio. "She was all over you last night; rare thing for Polly."

"Cute kid," reflected Wesley. He walked over to the window and sat on the ledge; pushing open a side pane, he glanced down at the street. It was a cool, sunny morning. The brownstone buildings, reminders of an older New York, stood in deep brown against a sky of magic blue; a pink-winged breeze breathed in through the open window. A faint sea-tang filled the new morning.

The radio began to play a Bing Crosby ballad. Wesley swept his gaze down the street and saw the Hudson in the clear distance, a mirrored sheen specked with merchant ships.

Everhart was standing beside him: "What do you do, Wes?"

Wesley pointed toward the ships on the river.

Everhart gazed in the same direction: "You're a merchant seaman are you?"

Wesley nodded as he offered his friend a cigarette; they lit up in silence.

"How is it?" inquired Everhart.

Wesley turned his brown eyes on Bill: "I try to make it my home," he said.

"Lonely sort of business, isn't it?"

"Yeah," admitted Wesley, emitting a double tendril of smoke from his nose.

"I always thought about the sea and ships and that sort of thing," said Everhart, his eyes fixed on the distant ships. "Get away from all this baloney."

They heard women's laughter from the bedrooms, rich bursts of confidential mirth that precipitated a sheepish grin on Everhart's face: "The gals are up; now what in heavens are they laughing about?"

"Women always laugh that way," smiled Wesley.

"Isn't it the truth?" agreed Everhart. "Gets my goat oftentimes; wonder if they're laughing at me . . ."

Wesley smiled at Everhart: "Why should they man?"

Everhart laughed as he removed his heavy glasses to polish them; he looked quite younger without them: "Tell you one thing, though; no finer sound in the morning than women laughing in the next room!"

Wesley opened his mouth and widened his eyes in his characteristic silent laughter.

"Whose apartment is this?" Wesley presently asked, throwing his cigarette butt in the street below.

"It's Eve's," responded Everhart, adjusting his spectacles. "She's a drunkard."

From the next room Polly's voice called out in a hurt way: "Is my Wesley gone away?"

"No he's still here," called back Everhart.

"That's my honey!" asserted Polly from the next room.

Wesley smiled from his seat at the window. Everhart approached him: "Why don't you go on in?"

"Had enough. That's all I been doing for two weeks," confided Wesley.

Everhart laughed heartily. At the radio, he tuned for a while until he found a satisfactory program.

"Battle Hymn of the Republic," informed Everhart. "Great old tune, isn't it? What does it make you think of?"

They both listened for awhile, until Wesley made his answer; "Abe Lincoln and the Civil War, I guess."

Ginger swept into the room and gasped: "My Gawd! Will you look at this room!" It was, indeed, a sorry sight: chairs were turned over, bottles, glasses, and cocktail mixers were strewn everywhere, and a vase had been broken near the couch. "I'll have to improve this mess somewhat before I go to work," she added, more or less to herself. "How do you feel, Shortypants?" she asked of Everhart. Then, without a pause for his response: "Wes! You look absolutely tip-top there? Haven't you got a big head?"

Wesley nodded toward Everhart: "He gave me a bromo. I feel right fine."

"Right fine," echoed Everhart. "I heard that expression last time . . ."

"George is still sleeping!" interrupted Ginger, bustling around picking up the bottles and things. "He's a lazy old slop."

"Last time I heard 'right fine' was down in Charlotte, North Carolina," continued Everhart. "They also used to say, when you wanted to know where something was, that it was 'right yonder,' I thought you were from Vermont, Wes?"

"I am," smiled Wesley. "I been all over this country though; spent two years in the south. Them expressions just come to me."

"Been to California?" asked Everhart.

"All over the place—forty-three states. I guess I missed Dakota, Missouri, Ohio and a few others."

"What were you doing, just loafing around?" inquired Everhart.

"I worked here and there."

"My goodness, it's already ten o'clock!" discovered Ginger. "Let's eat some breakfast right away! I've got to beat it!"

"Do you have any eggs?" asked Everhart.

"Oh, hell, no! Eve and I finished them yesterday morning."

Polly entered the room in Ginger's bathrobe, smiling after a shower: "I feel better," she announced. "Mornin' Wesley!" She walked to his side and puckered her lips: "Kiss me!" Wesley planted a brief kiss on her lips, then slowly blew a cloud of smoke into her face.

"Give me a drag!" demanded Polly, reaching for his cigarette.

"I'll go down and buy some eggs and fresh coffee buns," Everhart told Ginger. "Make some fresh coffee."

"Okay!"

"Coming with me, Wes?" called Everhart.

Wesley ruffled Polly's hair and rose to his feet: "Right!"

"Come right back," said Polly, peering slant-eyed through a cloud of cigarette smoke with a small seductive smile.

"Back right soon!" cried Everhart, slapping Wesley on the back.

In the automatic elevator, they could still hear the strains of the "Battle Hymn of the Republic" coming from Eve's radio.

"That song makes you think of Abe Lincoln and the Civil War," remembered Everhart. "It does me too, but it also makes me mad. I want to know what the hell went wrong, and who it was inflicted the wrong." The elevator stopped on the ground floor and slid open its doors. "That old cry 'America! America' What in heavens happened to its meaning. It's as though an America is just that—America—a beautiful word for a beautiful world—until people just simply come to its shores, fight the savage natives, develop it, grow rich, and then lean back to yawn and belch. God, Wes, if you were an assistant instructor in English Literature as I am, with its songs, songs ever saying: 'Go on! Go on!' and then you look over your class, look out of the window, and there's your America, your songs, your pioneer's cry to brave the West—a roomful of bored bastards, a grimy window facing Broadway with its meat markets and barrooms and God knows the rest. Does this mean frontiers from now on are to be in the imagination?"

Wesley, it is to be admitted, was not listening too closely: he was not quite certain as to what his friend rambled on about. They were now in the street. Ahead, a colored man was busy disposing of a black pile of coal down a hole in the sidewalk: the coal flashed back the sun's morning brilliance like a black hill studded with gems.

"It certainly does," Everhart assured himself. "And there is promise in that: but no more romance! No more buckskins and long rifles and coonskins and hot buttered rum at Fort Dearborn, no more trails along the river, no more California. That state is the end of it; if California had stretched around the world back to New England, we might have driven west eternally, rediscovering and re-building and moving on until civilization would assume the aspects of a six-day bike race with new possibilities at each bend. . . ."

Wesley, walking around the coal pile with his talkative friend, addressed the man with the shovel.

"Hey there, Pops! Don't work too hard!"

The man looked up and smiled happily: "Watch out there, man!" he shouted with whooping delight, leaning on his shovel. "You is talkin' out mah league—I doan split no gut! Hoo hoo hoo!"

"That's the ticket, Pops!" said Wesley, looking back with a smile.

"I swear to God," resumed Everhart, adjusting his glasses, "if this were 1760 I'd be on my way West with the trappers, explorers, and the huntsmen! I'm not rugged, the Lord knows, but I want a life with purpose, with a driving force and a mighty one at that. Here I am at Columbia, teaching—what of it? I accomplish nothing; my theories are accepted and that's all there is to it. I have seen how ideas are accepted and set aside for reference . . . that is why I gave up writing a long time ago. I'm thirty-two now; I wouldn't write a book for a million. There's no sense to it. Those lynx-eyed explorers—they were the American poets! The great unconscious poets who saw hills to the westward and were satisfied and that was that: they didn't have to rhapsodize, their very lives did that with more power than a Whitman! Do you read much, Wes?"

The were now on Broadway, strolling along the spacious pavement; Wesley stopped to peel his orange over a city refuse basket, and after a pause during which he frowned with dark pity, he said: "I used to know a young seaman by the name of Lucian Smith; he used to try to make me read, because I never did do much reading." He dropped the last peel in the basket with a slow, thoughtful flourish. "Luke finally made me read a book; he was a good kid and I wanted to make him feel as though he done me a favor. So I read the book he gave me."

"What was it?"

"*Moby Dick*," recollected Wesley.

"By Herman Melville," added Everhart, nodding his head.

Wesley tore the orange in two and offered a half to his friend. They walked on, eating. "So I read *Moby Dick*; I read it slow, about five pages a night, because I knew the kid would ask me questions about it."

"Did you like it?" Everhart asked.

Wesley spat out an orange grain, the same grave frown on his countenance: "Yeah," he answered.

"What did the Smith kid ask you about it?" persisted Everhart.

Wesley turned his troubled face on the interrogator and stared for a few moments.

"All kinds of questions," he finally told him. "All kinds. He was a bright kid."

"Do you remember any of his questions?" Everhart smiled, conscious of his inquisitiveness.

Wesley shrugged: "Not offhand."

"Where is he now?"

"The kid?"

"Yes . . ."

Wesley's frown disappeared; in its place, an impassive, almost defiant stoniness manifested itself in his averted face.

"Lucian Smith, he went down."

Everhart shot a scowling look toward his companion: "You mean he was torpedoed and drowned?" Everhart said this as though incredulous of such a thing; he rushed on: "He's dead now? When did it happen? Why did . . . where was it?"

Wesley thrust his hand in his back pocket, saying: "Off Greenland last January." He produced his seaman's wallet, a large flat affair with a chain attached. "Here's his picture," he announced, handing Bill a small snapshot: "Smith's a good kid."

Everhart, taking the snapshot, was going to say something, but checked himself nervously. A sad face gazed out at him from the photograph, but he was too confused to make anything further of it: Wesley's brooding presence, the sounds of the street gathering tempo for a new day, the gay sunshine's warmth, and the music from a nearby radio store all seemed to remove this pinched little face with the sad eyes to a place far off, lonely, and forgotten, to unreal realm that was as inconsequential as the tiny bit of celluloid paper he held between his fingers. Bill handed back the picture and could say nothing. Wesley did not look at the picture, but slid it back into his wallet, saying: "Where do we buy the eggs?"

"Eggs . . ." echoed Everhart, adjusting his spectacles slowly. "Up ahead two blocks."

On the way back, laden with packages, they said very little. In front of a bar, Wesley pointed toward it and smiled faintly: "Come on, man, let's go in and have a little breakfast."

Everhart followed his companion into the cool gloom of the bar, with its washed aroma and smell of fresh beer, and sat near the window where the sun poured in through the French blinds in flat strips. Wesley ordered two beers. Everhart glanced down and noticed his friend wore no socks beneath his moccasin shoes; they rested on the brass rail with the calm that seemed part of his whole being.

"How old are you, Wes?"

"Twenty-seven."

"How long have you been going to sea?"

The beers were placed before them by a morose bartender; Bill threw a quarter on the mahogany top of the bar.

"Six years now," answered Wesley, lifting the golden glass to the sun and watching the effervescence of many minute bubbles as they shot upward.

"Been leading a pretty careless life, haven't you?" Everhart went on. "Port debaucheries, then back to sea; and on that way . . ."

"That's right."

"You'd never care to plant some roots in society, I suppose," mused the other.

"Tried it once, tried to plant some roots, as you say . . . I had a wife and a kid coming, my job was a sure thing, we had a house." Wesley halted himself and drank down the bitter thoughts. But he resumed: "Split up after the kid died stillborn, all that sort of guff: I hit the road, bummed all over the U.S.A., finally took to shipping out."

Everhart listened sympathetically, but Wesley had said his piece.

"Well," sighed Bill slapping the bar, "I find myself, at thirty-two, an unusually free and fortunate man; but honestly I'm not happy."

"So what!" countered Wesley. "Bein' happy's O.K. in its place; but other things count more."

"That's the sort of statement I should make, or anyone of the creative artists whose works I talk on," considered the other, "but as for you, a doubtlessly devil-may-care roué with a knack for women and a triple capacity for liquor, it seems strange. Aren't you happy when you're blowing your pay in port?"

Wesley waved a disgusted hand: "Hell no! What else can I do with money? I ain't got no one to send it to but my father and one of my married brothers, and when that's done, I still got too much money—I throw it away, practically. I'm not happy then."

"When are you happy?"

"Never, I guess; I get a kick out of a few things, but they don't last; I'm talkin' about the beach now."

"Then you are happy at sea?"

"Guess so . . . I'm home then anyway, and I know my work and what I'm doin'. I'm an A.B., see . . . but as to bein' happy at sea, I don't really know. Hell, what is happiness nohow?" Wesley asked with a trace of scorn.

"No such thing?" suggested Bill.

"You hoppin' skippin' Goddamn right!" asserted Wesley, smiling and shaking his head.

Bill called for two more beers.

"My old man is a bartender in Boston," confided Wesley. "He's a great old buck."

"My old man used to be a shipyard worker," Everhart supplied, "but now he's old and feeble; he's sixty-two. I take care of him and my kid brother financially, while my married sister, who lives in my place with her crum of a husband, feeds and cares [for] them. The kid goes to public school—he's a doughty little brat."

Wesley listened to this without comment.

"I'd like to make a change; spread my wings and see if they are ready for flight," confessed Bill. "Know something? . . . I'd like to try the Merchant Marine for a spell!"

"How about your draft status?" Wesley asked.

"Just registered so far, unless my notification came in this morning's mail," pondered Bill. "But by heavens I really would like the idea!" Everhart lapsed into a musing silence while the other lit up a cigarette and inspected the glowing tip. He could use a little money, considering that the old man would soon require a hernia operation. What was it the doctor had said? . . . seven months? And the kid might want to go to Columbia in five or six years.

"How much money can you make on a trip?" asked Bill at length.

Wesley, with a mouthful of beer, held it for a moment, tasting it with relish.

"Well," he answered, "depends. You'd make a bit less as ordinary seaman. The Russian run would net you around fourteen hundred bucks in five or six months, with pay, sea bonus, port bonus, and overtime. But a short run, like the Iceland or coastwise to Texas or South American run wouldn't add up to that much in one trip."

Well, two or three short trips, or one long one would certainly make a tidy sum. Everhart, who made thirty dollars a week at Columbia, sharing the rent with his sister's husband, had always had enough money, but never enough to realize any savings or lay the foundations for future security. He often managed to make a few extra dollars tutoring private students at examination time. But since 1936, when he was awarded his master's degree in English and was fortunate enough to land an assistant professorship in the university, he had more or less coasted along, spending whatever money he kept for himself and living out a life of harangue with students, professors, and people like George Day; living, in short, a casually civilized New York City existence. He had studied hard and proved a brilliant student. But the restlessness which had festered in his loquacious being through the years as assistant professor in English, a vague prod in the course of his somehow sensationless and self-satisfied days, now came to him in a rush of accusal. What was he doing with his life? He had never grown attached to any woman, outside of the gay and promiscuous relations he carried on with several young ladies in the vicinity of his circle. Others at the university, he now considered with a tinge of remorse, had grown properly academic, worn good clothes with the proud fastidiousness of young professors, gotten themselves wives, rented apartments on or near the campus, and set about to lead serious, purposeful lives with an eye to promotions and honorary degrees and a genuine affection for their wives and children.

But he had rushed around for the past six years clad in his cloak of genius, an enthusiastic young pedant with loud theories, shabby clothing, and a barefaced conviction in the art of criticism. He'd never paused to appraise anything but the world. He had never really paid any attention to his own life, except to use his own freedom as a means to discuss the subject of freedom. Yes, he was Everhart who had told his classes, one triumphant morning when the snow lashed against the windows, that art was the revolt of the free. . . .

Theories! Lectures! Talk! Thirty dollars per week; home in the evening, while the old man snored in his chair, correcting papers and preparing lecture notes; down at the bar with George Day, studying for his master's, talking over beers and making wry observations on everything; plays, concerts, operas, lectures; rushing around carrying books shouting hellos to everyone; weekend wild parties with various acquaintances; then back to Sunday—the *Times*, those fine dinners of his sister's, arguments at the table with her radio store owner of a husband, damn his smug hide, and a movie with Sonny at night in the Nemo, full of Columbia College students throwing things from the balcony. Then back to Monday morning, a class, a quick lunch at the Sandwich shop, reference work in the afternoon seated in the library, a quick beer before supper, and a lecture by Ogden Nash in McMillin at eight-thirty. Then back to the bar for a quick beer, long discussions with the boys—Day, Purcell, Fitzgerald, Gobel, Allen . . . as drunken a mob of pseudo-scholars as he was ever privileged to behold—and finally home to a dying old father, a busybody sister, a self-appointed humorist of a brother-in-law, a noisy kid brother, and a horrible looking poodle dog.

Bah! Then Everhart retires, placing his horn-rimmed glasses on the dresser, and stretches his pudgy frame in the bed and wonders what the hell it's all leading to!

Well, now it had come to this; at thirty-two, a queer-looking assistant professor, known amiably around the whole place as "Shortypants." The price of trying to be unpretentious! Do like the others, radiate professorial dignity, and they will call you William or Professor Everhart. To hell with it!

Lost? That poet's word . . .

"Thinkin' of shipping out?" Wesley interrupted the other's reverie.

Everhart directed a scowl toward him, still lost in his own thoughts; but he finally answered: "If only for a change, yes."

"Let's have another beer," suggested Wesley.

Everhart had to laugh: "We'd better be getting back, the girls are waiting for the eggs and us."

Wesley waved a scoffing hand.

They had more beer; and more. In forty-five minutes or so, they each consumed eight glasses of cold, needling ale. They decided to go back. Everhart felt decidedly tingling by this time. All through breakfast he told them all he was shipping out with Wesley, repeating his decision at measured intervals. George Day, who had by this time risen, sat eating his breakfast with an ill-tempered scowl, munching quite noisily and with no acknowledgement of the presence of the others.

Everhart, feeling quite gay from the beer, slapped George on the back and invited him to go shipping in the Merchant Marine with him. George turned up a drawn, rather gloomy countenance, and with the help of an already dour face, heavy with tired flesh, he made it known that he was averse to the suggestion.

Ginger drew a toast from the grill and laughed: "Don't you have a class this morning, Georgie?"

Day mumbled something that sounded like "Ancient History of the Near East and Greece."

"Poof!" scoffed Everhart, flourishing his fork, "Come with me and *see* the Near East."

George snuffed briefly down his nose and muttered through a mouthful of toast: "You don't think, do you Everhart, I'm taking the course because I want to know something about the Near East. The Near East is as dear to me as a glass of milk."

"Ha!" shouted Everhart. "Port Said! Alexandria! The Red Sea! There's your East . . . I'm going to see it!"

George belched quietly, excusing himself after a moment of afterthought.

Polly, perched on Wesley's lap, ruffled his hair and wanted to know if he had a cigarette. While Wesley drew a package from his coat pocket, the girl bit his ear and breathed warmly into it.

"Now, now Polly!" giggled Ginger.

After breakfast, Ginger shooed them all out and locked the door. She had worn a brown suit with stitched seams and double slit pockets in the jacket; beneath it she wore a casual sport shirt.

"This is the suit I have to model this morning," she chattered to all in general. "Twelve ninety-five. Don't you think it's cute?"

"No frills, no flubs!" commented Everhart.

"Could I get one cheap?" demanded Polly from Wesley's arm. "See how much you can get it for; I'll give you the money. I think it's classic!"

They were now in the street. George Day, very tall and shambling, dragged along behind them, not quite capable of maintaining any sort of morning dignity. Polly strode beside Wesley chatting gayly, while Ginger and Everhart talked through one another about what ever occurred to their minds. Near the 110th Street subway entrance Ginger left them. "Oh look!" cried George, pointing toward a bar across the street. Ginger, ready to cross the street, turned: "You go to your class, Day!" She ran off across the street for her subway, her trim little heels clacking a rapid staccato. "How," George wanted to know in general, "can a woman with legs like that be so cruel?" Near 114th Street, George left them with a brief "Goodbye kids" and shuffled off toward his class, hands dug reluctantly in his pockets.

"A gentleman and a pseudo-scholar," Everhart observed. A group of girls in slacks walked by in the warm sunlight, laden with tennis rackets and basketballs, their multi-colored heads of hair radiant in the morning glitter. Wesley appraised them with a frank stare. When one of the girls whistled, Polly whistled back. Near a small cigar store, a tall curly haired youth and another shorter one with glasses, paid their respects to Polly with a rhythmic whistle that kept in time with her long, loose stride. Polly whistled back to them.

They turned down 116th Street toward the Drive.

"I'd better be getting home or my aunt will brain me," said Polly, laughing on Wesley's lapel.

"Where do you live?" asked Wesley.

"On the Drive, near the Delta Chi house," she told him. "Look, Wes, where are you going now?"

Wesley turned to Everhart.

"He's coming with me," said the latter. "I'm going home and breaking the news to the folks. I don't have to ask them, but I want to see if it's all right with them."

"Bill, are you really joining the Merchant Marine? I thought you were just drunk!" confessed Polly with a laugh.

"Why not?" barked Everhart. "I want to get away from all this for awhile."

"What about the University?" Polly supplied.

"That's no problem; all I have to do is ask for a vacation. I've been at it for six years without a break; they'll certainly grant me the request."

Polly returned her attention to Wesley: "Well, Wes, I'm expecting you to call on me at six tonight—no, I make it seven, I have to get a manicure at Mae's. We'll have another wild time. Do you know any good places we could hit tonight?"

"Sure," smiled Wesley, "I always have a right big time down in Harlem; I got some friends there, some boys I used to ship with."

"That's swell!" sang Polly. "We can go there; I'd like to see a show before, though; let's go downtown to the Paramount and see Bob Hope."

Wesley shrugged: "Suits me, but I'm broke just now."

"Oh the hell with that, I can get some money from my aunt!" cried Polly. "What about you Bill? Want me to call Eve for you? I don't think she's doing anything tonight; Friday today, isn't it?"

"Yes," mused Bill. "We'll see about tonight; I'll call you up. I have to see Dean Stewart this afternoon about my leave." Everhart's face, wrinkled in thought and indecision, was turned toward the river. He could see a line of underwear strung along the aft deck of a tanker, and a tiny figure standing motionless beside the four-inch gun on a turret.

"I can see someone on that tanker," smiled Bill, pointing toward the distant anchored ship. "Why isn't he ashore having a good time?" They all gazed down the street toward the tanker.

"Too much fuss on the beach for him," affirmed Wesley in a strange, quiet voice. Everhart shot an inquisitive glance toward his companion.

"Wesley!" commanded Polly, "Pick me up at seven sharp; don't forget! I'll be waiting . . ." She backed away with a frown: "Okay?"

"Right," Wesley answered imperturbably.

"G'bye kids!" sang Polly; moving on down the street.

"So long," said Everhart, waving briefly.

"Adios," added Wesley.

Polly turned and shouted: "Seven tonight!"

Bill and Wesley crossed the street, halting while a dairy truck purred past. "I live right up here," indicated Everhart, pointing up Claremont Avenue. "Christ it's hot today!"

Wesley, hands in pockets, said nothing. A distinguished looking old gentleman walked by, nodding briefly at Everhart.

"Old man Parsons," revealed the latter.

Wesley smiled: "I'll be damned!"

Everhart smote the other on the back and chuckled goodnaturedly, reposing his hand for a moment on the thin shoulder: "You're a rare duck, Wes!"

CHAPTER THREE

We Are Brothers, Laughing

Everhart's home proved to be a dark, rambling hall leading to various rooms on each side. More books, magazines, and pamphlets than Wesley had ever seen were strewn everywhere in bookcases, on shelves, and on tables.

Bill's sister, a rather unceremonious woman in the midst of her house work, shouted at them over the whining roar of a vacuum cleaner to keep out of the sitting room. They walked down the dim, narrow hall to Bill's own bedroom, where books were evident in even more quantity and confusion than in the rest of the apartment. A spacious window opened on the green lawns and luxuriously leafed trees of the Barnard College campus, where several of the girl students sat chatting away their summer session.

"Here," said Everhart, handing Wesley a pair of binoculars, "see if you can detect any compromising postures down there."

Wesley's face lit up with silent mirth; binoculars to his eyes, his open mouth widened as the humor of the situation heightened his delight.

"Fine," he commented briefly, his silent laughter at length beginning to shake his thin frame.

Bill took the binoculars and peered seriously.

"Hmm," he admitted.

"That you Billy?" a man's voice called from the next room.

"Yeah!" called Everhart, adding to Wesley: "The old pater . . . wait a second."

When Bill had gone, Wesley picked up a notebook and glanced briefly through it. On the flyleaf, someone had written: "Give them Tom Wolfe the way he should be given—America's song in the 'Angel,' one of our best songs, growing from thence to satire—the satire of 'Hill Beyond,' not simply the bite of a Voltaire but the grandeur and beauty of a Swift; Wolfe, immense gangling freak of a man, striding Swift in our complacent midst!" On another page, figures were inscribed apparently a budget account, subtracting and adding themselves in a confused jumble. Beside the word 'operation' stood the sum of five hundred dollars.

Wesley picked up another notebook; it was full of references, subreferences, and notations; a photograph fell out from between the pages. Wesley glanced at it with the minute curiosity of his nature; a man stood before Grant's Tomb holding the hand of a small boy, while a plump woman stood nearby laughing. Underneath, in ink, a hand had scrawled the identities: Father, Billy, Mother—1916. Wesley studied the background, where busy little men strode past in the performance of their afternoon duties and ladies stood transfixed in gestures of enthusiasm, laughter, and curiosity.

Wesley replaced the faded brown picture with a slow, hesitant hand. For a long while, he stared sightlessly at the rug on the floor.

"Funny . . ." he muttered quietly.

From the next room, he could hear the low rumble of men's voices. Down in the street below the open window a baby wailed from its carriage; a girl's voice soothed in the noon stillness: "Geegee, geegee, stop crying."

Wesley went to the window and glanced down the street; way off in the distance, the clustered pile of New York's Medical Center stood, a grave healer surrounded at its hem by smaller buildings where the healed returned. From Broadway, a steady din of horns, trolley bells, grinding gears, and screeching trolley wheels surmounted the deeper, vaster hum from the high noon thoroughfare. It was very warm by now; a crazy haze danced toward the sun while a few of the more ambitious birds chattered in sleepy protest from the green. Wesley took off his coat and slouched into an easy chair by the window. When he was almost asleep, Everhart was talking to him: ". . . well, the old man leaves me my choice. All I have to do now is speak to my brother-in-law and to the Dean. You wait here, Wes, I'll call the jerk up . . . he's in his radio repair shop . . ."

Everhart was gone again. Wesley dozed off; once he heard a boy's voice speaking from the door: "Geez! Who's dat!": Later, Everhart was back, bustling through the confusion of papers and books on his desk.

"Where the hell? . . ."

Wesley preferred to keep his eyes closed; for the first time in two weeks, since he had signed off the last freighter, he felt content and at peace with himself. A fly lit on his nose, but he was too lazy to shoo it off; it left a moist little feeling when he twitched it away.

"Here it is!" muttered Everhart triumphantly, and he was off again.

Wesley felt a thrill of anticipation as he sat there dozing: in a few days, back on a ship, the sleepy thrum of the propeller churning in the water below, the soothing rise and fall of the ship, the sea stretching around the horizon, the rich, clean sound of the bow splitting water . . . and the long hours lounging on deck in the sun, watching the play of the clouds, ravished by the full, moist breeze. A simple life! A serious life! To make the sea your own, to watch over it, to brood your very soul into it, to accept it and love it as though only it mattered and existed! "A.B. Martin!" they called him. "He's a quiet good enough seaman, good worker," they would say of him. Hah! Did they know he stood on the bow every morning, noon, and night for an hour; did they suspect this profound duty of his, this prayer of thanks to a God more a God than any to be found in book-bound, altar-bound Religion?

Sea! Sea! Wesley opened his eyes, but closed them rapidly. He wanted to see the ocean as he had often seen it from his foc'sle porthole, a heaving world pitching high above the port, then dropping below to give a glimpse of the seasky—as wild and beautiful as the sea—and then the sea surging up again. Yes, he used to lay there in his bunk with a cigarette and a magazine, and for hours he would gaze at the porthole, and there was the surging sea, the receding sky. But now he could not see it; the image of Everhart's bedroom was etched there, clouding the clean, green sea.

But Wesley had felt the thrill, and it would not leave him: soon now, a spray-lashed day in the gray green North Atlantic, that most rugged and moody of oceans . . .

Wesley reached for a cigarette and opened his eyes; a cloud had come across the face of the sun, the birds had suddenly stopped, the street was gray and humid. An old man was coughing in the next room.

Everhart was back.

"Well!" he said. "Done, I guess . . ."

Wesley passed his hand through the thin black mat of his hair: "What's done?"

Everhart opened a dresser drawer: "You've been sleeping, my beauty. I saw the Dean, and it's all right with him; he thinks I'm going to the country for a vacation."

Everhart slapped a laundered shirt in his hand meditatively: "The noble brother-in-law whined until I made it clear I'd be back with enough money to pay up all the half-rents and half-boards in this country for a year. At the end, he was fairly enthusiastic . . ."

"What time is it?" yawned Wesley.

"One-thirty."

"Shuck-all! I've been sleepin' . . . and dreamin' too," said Wesley, drawing deep from his cigarette.

Everhart approached Wesley's side. "Well, Wes," he began, "I'm going with you—or that is, I'm shipping out. Do you mind if I follow you along? I'm afraid I'd be lost alone, with all the union hall and papers business . . ."

"Hell no, man!" Wesley smiled. "Ship with me!"

"Let's shake on that!" smiled the other, proffering his hand. Wesley wrung his hand with grave reassurance.

Everhart began to pack with furious energy, laughing and chatting. Wesley told him he knew of a ship in Boston bound for Greenland, and that getting one's Seaman's papers was a process of several hours' duration. They also planned to hitchhike to Boston that very afternoon.

"Look!" cried Everhart, brandishing his binoculars. "These will be more useful from a deck!" He threw them into the suitcase, laughing.

"You don't need much stuff," observed Wesley. "I'm gonna get me a toothbrush in Boston."

"Well at least I'm going to bring some good books along," Everhart cried enthusiastically, hurling dozens of Everyman volumes into his pack. "Greenland!" he cried. "What's it like up there, Wes?"

"I ain't seen it; that's why I want to go."

"I'll bet it's a God-forsaken place!"

Wesley flipped his cigarette through the open window: "Never saw Greenland, been to Russia and Iceland; Africa in 1936, eleven ports on the Gold coast; China, India, Liverpool, Gibraltar, Marseilles, Trinidad, Japan,

Sidney, hell's shuck-all, I been all the way to hell and gone and back."

Sonny Everhart, a boy of ten years, entered and stared at Wesley: "Are you the guy what's the sailor Bill's goin' wit?"

"This is my kid brother," explained Bill, opening the closet door. "Don't pay any attention to him; he's a brat!"

Sonny squared off to box his big brother, but he only waved a playful arm and went back to his packing.

"He thinks he's tough," announced Sonny. "One more year and I'll lick him easy." To prove this, he vaulted over the back of an easy chair groaning with books and landed on his feet to stand poised and indifferent.

"Let's feel your muscles," offered Wesley.

Sonny walked over and flexed his little arm. Wesley wrapped a thin brown hand around it and winked knowingly, nodding toward the older brother.

"Six months most," he reassured Sonny.

Sonny laughed savagely. Wesley rose to his feet and put on his coat slowly.

"D'jever see a German?" asked Sonny.

Wesley sat down on the edge of the large chair. "Sure," he said.

"Did he try to shoot you?"

"No; this was before the war," explained Wesley.

Sonny jumped on the seat, landing on his knees. "Even then!" he cried.

"Nope," said Wesley.

"D'jever see a submarine?"

"Yup."

"Where?"

"I seen one off Cape Hatteras; they sunk our ship," he returned.

"What you do?" shrilled Sonny.

"I jumped over the poop deck, feller."

"Ha ha! What a name for a deck! Poop!"

Wesley's eyes widened in silent laughter; he placed his hand on Sonny's head and rolled it slowly, growling. Sonny leaped back and slapped his hips: "Brah! Brah!" he barked, pointing his forefingers. Wesley clutched his breast and staggered over.

"Brah! Brah! Brah! Full o' holes!" informed Sonny, sitting on the bed.

Wesley lit up another cigarette and threw the empty pack in the waste basket. The sun was back, spilling its warmth into the room in a sudden dazzle of afternoon gold.

"My Pop used to fix ships," Sonny continued. "Did you ever see my Pop?"

"No," confessed Wesley.

"C'mon," urged Sonny. "He's right here."

Everhart, busy rummaging in the closet, made no remarks, so Wesley followed Sonny into the dim hall and into another room.

This particular room faced the inner court of the building, so that no sun served to brighten what ordinarily would be a gloomy chamber in the first place. A large man clad in a brown bathrobe sat by the window smoking a pipe. The room was furnished with a large bed, an easy chair (in which the father sat), another smaller chair, a dresser, a battered trunk, and an ancient radio with exterior loudspeaker and all. From this radio there now emitted a faint strain of music through a clamor of static.

"Hey Paw!" sang Sonny. "Here's that sailor!"

The man turned from his revery and fixed two red-rimmed eyes on them, half stunned. Then he perceived Wesley and smiled a pitifully twisted smile, waving his hand in salute.

Wesley waved back, greeting: "Hullo!"

"How's the boy?" Mr. Everhart wanted to know, in a deep, gruff, workingman's voice.

"Fine," Wesley said.

"Billy's goin' with you, hey?" the father smiled, his mouth twisted down into a chagrined pout, as though to smile was to admit defeat. "I always knew the little cuss had itchy feet."

Wesley sat down on the edge of the bed while Sonny ran to the foot of the bed to preside over them proudly.

"This's my youngest boy," said the father of Sonny, "I'd be a pretty lonely man without him. Everybody else seems to have forgotten me." He coughed briefly. "Your father alive, son?" he resumed.

Wesley leaned a hand on the mottled bedspread: "Yeah . . . he's in Boston."

"Where's your people from?"

"Vermont originally."

"Vermont? What part?"

"Bennington," answered Wesley, "my father owned a service station there for twenty-two years."

"Bennington," mused the old man, nodding his head in recollection. "I traveled through there many years ago. Long before your time."

"His name's Charley Martin," supplied Wesley.

"Martin? . . . I used to know a Martin from Baltimore, a Jack Martin he was."

There was a pause during which Sonny slapped the bedstead. Outside, the sun faded once more, plunging the room into a murky gloom. The radio sputtered with static.

Bill's sister entered the room, not even glancing at Wesley.

"Is Bill in his room?" she demanded.

The old man nodded: "He's packing his things, I guess."

"Packing his things?" she cried. "Don't tell me he's really going through with his silly idea?"

Mr. Everhart shrugged.

"For God's sake, Pa, are you going to let him do it?"

"It's none of my business—he has a mind of his own," returned the old man calmly, turning toward the window.

"He has a mind of his own!" she mimicked savagely.

"Yes he has!" roared the old man, spinning around to face his daughter angrily, "I can't stop him."

She tightened her lips irritably for a moment.

"You're his father aren't you!" she shouted.

"Oh!" boomed Mr. Everhart with a vicious leer. "So now I'm the father of the house!"

The woman stamped out of the room with an outraged scoff.

"That's a new one!" thundered the father after her.

Sonny snickered mischievously.

"That's a new one!" echoed the old man to himself. "They dumped me in this back room years ago when I couldn't work any more and forgot all about it. My word in this house hasn't meant anything for years."

Wesley fidgeted nervously with the hem of the old quilt blanket.

"You know, son," resumed Mr. Everhart with a sullen scowl, "a man's useful in life so long's he's producin' the goods, bringin' home the bacon; that's when he's Pop, the breadwinner, and his word is the word of the house. No sooner he grows old an' sick an' can't work any more, they flop him up in some odd corner o' the house," gesturing at his room, "and forget all about him, unless it be to call him a damn nuisance."

From Bill's room they could hear arguing voices.

"I ain't stoppin' him from joining the merchant marine if that's what he wants," grumbled the old man. "And I know damn well I couldn't stop him if I wanted to, so there!" He shrugged wearily.

Wesley tried to maintain as much impartiality as he could; he lit a cigarette nervously and waited patiently for a chance to get out of this uproarious household. He wished he had waited for Bill at a nice cool bar.

"I suppose it's none too safe at sea nowadays," reflected Mr. Everhart aloud.

"Not exactly," admitted Wesley.

"Well, Bill will have to face danger sooner or later, Army or Navy or merchant marines. All the youngsters are in for it," he added dolefully. "Last war, I tried to get in but they refused me—wife n'kids. But this is a different war, all the boys are going in this one."

The father laid aside his pipe on the window sill, leaning over with wheezing labor. Wesley noticed he was quite fat; the hands were powerful, though, full of veinous strength, the fingers gnarled and enormous.

"Nothin' we can do," continued Mr. Everhart. "We people of the common herd are to be seen but not heard. Let the big Money Bags start the wars, we'll fight 'em and love it." He lapsed into a malign silence.

"But I got a feelin'," resumed the old man with his pouting smile, "that Bill's just goin' along for the fun. He's not one you can fool, Billy . . . and I guess he figures the merchant marine will do him some good, whether he takes only one trip or not. Add color to his cheeks, a little sea an' sunshine. He's been workin' pretty hard all these years. Always a quiet little duck readin' books by himself. When the woman died from Sonny, he was twenty-two, a senior in the College—hit him hard, but he managed. I was still workin' at the shipyards, so I sent him on for more degrees. The daughter offered to move in with her husband an' take care of little Sonny. When Billy finished his education—I always knew education was a good thing—I swear I wasn't surprised when he hit off a job with the Columbia people here."

Wesley nodded.

The father leaned forward anxiously in his chair.

"Billy's not a one for the sort of thing he's goin' into now," he said with a worried frown. "You look like a good strong boy, son, and you've been through all this business and know how to take care of yourself. I hope . . . you keep an eye on Billy—you know what I mean—he's not . . ."

"Whatever I could do," assured Wesley, "I'd sure-all do it."

"Yes, because I'd feel better if I knew someone experienced was sorta keepin' an eye on him . . . you know what I mean, son."

"Sure do," answered Wesley.

"It's the way a father feels," apologized the old man. "You'll find out how it is someday when your own kids go off like this . . . it's something that can make you feel downright unhappy, and mad too, by God. I've come to the point where I can't understand it any more—I mean the whole blamed thing. You start off with a rosy-cheeked little kiddie, then he grows up, and the next thing y'know, he's standing face to face with you an' arguing his head off, and then he's gone . . . gone in more ways than one."

Bill was standing in the doorway.

"Oh Pa, for God's sake, stop telling all your troubles to my friends," he admonished.

The old man swung his chair around to the window and muttered bitterly. Bill's mouth hardened impatiently.

"We were havin' a right nice chat," Wesley said, a bit coldly.

"All right, I'm sorry," confessed Bill with some reluctance. "This is no way to say au revoir." He walked over to his father's chair: "well, old man, I guess you won't have me around to argue with for a while, I'll bet you'll miss me just the same." He leaned over and kissed his father's bristly cheek.

"Sure your doin' the right thing I guess," said Mr. Everhart, still facing his window.

"Well, we can use the money, right?"

The father shrugged. Then he turned and squeezed Bill's arm with his big hand: "If I could see you to the subway I would. Goodbye, Billy, an' be careful."

When Wesley shook hands with Mr. Everhart, his red-rimmed eyes were vague and misty.

"I'm goin' wid youse!" howled Sonny, back in Bill's room.

"Yeah, yeah!" cried Bill. "Go in the living room for awhile will you, Sonny: Wes and I want to talk. Tell Sis I'm coming out in a minute."

Sonny dashed off at a furious pace.

"First thing is to get a subway to the Bronx and start hitch-hiking along Route One, right?"

Wesley nodded.

"I wish I had fare money," growled Bill, "but I spent all my money last night. And I'm not borrowing any money from anyone, let alone my brother-in-law."

"Hell, man, we'll bum to Boston," said Wesley.

"Sure!" beamed the other. "Besides, I never hitch-hiked before; it would be an experience."

"Do we move?"

Everhart paused for a moment. What was he doing here in this room, this room he had known since childhood, this room he had wept in, had ruined his eyesight in, studying till dawn, this room into which his mother had often stole to kiss and console him, what was he doing in this suddenly sad room, his foot on a packed suitcase and a traveler's hat perched foolishly on the back of his head? Was he leaving it? He glanced at the old bed and suddenly realized that he would no longer sleep on that old downy mattress, long nights sleeping in safety. Was he forsaking this for some hard bunk on board a ship plowing through waters he had never hoped to see, a sea where ships and men were cheap and the submarine prowled like some hideous monster in DeQuincey's dreams. The whole thing failed to focus in his mind; he proved unable to meet the terror which this sudden contrast brought to bear on his soul. Could it be he knew nothing of life's great mysteries? Then what of the years spent interpreting the literatures of England and America for note-hungry classes? . . . had he been talking through his hat, an utterly complacent and ignorant little pittypat who spouted the profound feelings of a Shakespeare, a Keats, a Milton, a Whitman, a Hawthorne, a Melville, a Thoreau, a Robinson as though he knew the terror, fear, agony, and vowing passion of their lives and was brother to them in the dark, deserted old moor of their minds?

Wesley waited while Everhart stood in indecision, patiently attending to his fingernails. He knew his companion was hesitating.

At this moment, however, Bill's sister entered the room smoking a Fatima and still carrying her cup of tea. She and her friend, a middle-aged woman who now stood beaming in the doorway, had been engaged in passing the afternoon telling each other's fortunes in the tea leaves. Now the sister, a tall woman with a trace of oncoming middle age in her stern but youthful features, spoke reproachfully to her younger brother; "Bill, can't I do anything to change your mind. This is all so silly? Where are you going, for God's sake . . . be sensible."

"I'm only going on a vacation," growled Bill in a hunted manner. "I'll be back." He picked up his bag and leaned to kiss her on the cheek.

The sister sighed and adjusted his coat lapel. She glanced in a none too friendly fashion at Wesley, while he, in turn, wanted to tell her it was none of his doing and that would she kindly keep her dirty looks to herself?

In the street, Wesley could still see the old man, Mr. Everhart, as he had been when they had gone past his room on the way out: he was still sitting in the chair, but his pipe had lain unsmoked on the sill, a crest fallen, lonely figure.

At the subway, Sonny began to sniffle, but Bill gave him a quarter and told him to buy a Superman book. And just as they were going through the turnstiles, an associate of Bill's, a thin, nervous Englishman carrying two brief-cases and a book, shouted brightly above the heads of the subway goers: "I say Everhart! A vacation is it?"

"Yes," answered Bill.

"Lucky scoundrel!" was the reply, and the young man swayed off, his long neck loosely fitted to a gangling collar, striding purposefully toward an afternoon lecture.

In the subway, Bill was frightened; Wesley was so quiet Bill could hardly expect any sort of spiritual sympathy from him. Didn't the dammed fool know what was going on? . . . What folly was perhaps being committed? . . . what agony this impetuous change was already assuming? . . . and yet, too, what a coward "shortypants" was proving to be!

At this point, Everhart almost made up his mind to go back, but just then he remembered Wesley's date with Polly for that evening.

"What about your date with Polly?" Everhart asked half morosely, fiddling nervously with the handle of his suitcase. The train was roaring through its dark tunnel—people were reading their newspapers and chewing with bovine calm on wads of gum.

Wesley leaned over nearer, placing his hand on Bill's shoulder: "What d'you say?"

"What about your date with Polly?"

Wesley's mouth parted and his eyes widened with delight. Smacking Everhart resoundingly on the back, he shouted for the first time since Everhart had known him: "Who gives a good hoppin' shuckall?!!" he whooped in a rich, good humored, rakish howl. "We're shippin' out, man!!"

Everhart could still feel the sting in his back as the people in the subway peered curiously at Wesley, who now sat returning their stares with a roguish, wide-eyed humor, and quite amused.

Everhart leaned back and laughed heartily; he couldn't stop, and in his mind a voice was reproaching him as he laughed and laughed.

It said: "Is it the damned fool, who, at that dark moment, laughs courage right into you."

CHAPTER FOUR

At three o'clock, they were standing at the side of the road near Bronx Park; where cars rushed past fanning hot clouds of dust into their faces. Bill sat on his suitcase while Wesley stood impassively selecting cars with his experienced eye and raising a thumb to them. Their first ride was no longer than a mile, but they were dropped at an advantageous point on the Boston Post Road.

The sun was so hot Bill suggested a respite; they went to a filling station and drank four bottles of Coca-Cola. Bill went behind to the washroom. From there he could see a field and a fringe of shrub steaming in the July sun. He was on his way! . . . New fields, new roads, new hills were in store for him—and his destinations was the seacoast of old New England. What was the strange new sensation lurked in his heart, a fiery tingle to move on and discover anew the broad secrets of the world? He felt like a boy again . . . perhaps, too, he was acting a bit silly about the whole thing.

Back on the hot flank of the road, where the tar steamed its black fragrance, they hitched a ride almost immediately. The driver was a New York florist en route to his greenhouse near Portchester, N.Y. He talked volubly, a good-natured Jewish merchant with a flair for humility and humor: "A couple of wandering Jews!" he called them, smiling with a sly gleam in his pale blue eyes. He dropped them off a mile beyond his destinations on the New York-Connecticut state line.

Bill and Wesley stood beside a rocky bed which had been cut neatly at the side of the highway. In the shimmering distance, Connecticut's flat meadows stretched a pale green mat for sleeping trees.

Wesley took off his coat and hung it to a shoulder while Bill pushed his hat down over his eyes. They took turns sitting on the suitcase while the other leaned on the cliffside, proffering a lazy thumb. Great trucks labored up the hill, leaving behind a dancing shimmer of gasoline fumes.

"Next to the smell of salt water," drawled Wesley with a grassblade in his mouth, "I'll take the smell of a highway." He spat quietly with his lips. "Gasoline, tires, tar, and shrubbery," added Bill lazily. "Whitman's song of the open road, modern version." They sunned quietly, without comment, in the sudden stillness. Down the road, a truck was shifting into second gear to start its up-hill travails.

"Watch this," said Wesley. "Pick up your suitcase and follow me."

As the truck approached, now in first gear, Wesley waved at the driver and made as if to run alongside the slowly toiling behemoth. The driver, a colorful bandana around his neck, waved a hand in acknowledgement. Wesley tore the suitcase from Bill's hand and shouted: "Come on!" He dashed up to the truck and leaped onto the running board, shoving the suitcase into the cab and holding the door open, balanced on one foot, for Bill. The latter hung on to his hat and ran after the truck; Wesley gave him [a] hand as he plunged into the cab.

"Whoo!" cried Bill, taking off his hat. "That was a neat bit of Doug Fairbanks dash!" Wesley swung in beside him and slammed the door to.

"That'll melt the fat off!" roared the truck driver. "Hot as a sonofabitch, ain't it?" His laughter bellowed above the thunder of the motor.

They roared and careened all the way to New Haven, traveling at a furious pace downhill and crawling with a mounting whine uphill. When the driver dropped them off at the Yale University green, the sunlight had softened to a pale orange.

"Don't take any wooden nickels!" counseled the truck driver, bellowing above the crash of his gears as he left them in his thunderous wake.

"What now?" asked Everhart. They were standing on a broad pavement swarming with shoppers bearing packages, men in shirtsleeves en route from work, sauntering Yale summer students, newsboys, and business men. The street was a tangle of autos, buses, and clanging trolleys. The Green was a pageant of loafers.

"First thing is to get the hell out of here," muttered Wesley, moving off.

"When do we eat?"

"We'll eat in Hartford," said Wesley. "How much money did you say you had?"

"Three bucks or so."

"I'll borrow some when we hit Boston," mumbled Wesley. "Come on."

They took a State Street trolley and rode to the end of the line. They walked up the street for a few blocks and set up their hitchhiking post in front of a bakery. After fifteen minutes of thumbing, an agrarian looking old gentleman picked them up in his ancient Buick; all the way to Meriden, while the sun changed its color to a somber, burning orange and the meadows cooled to a clean, dark, and jungle green, the farmer carried on a monologue on the subject of farm prices, farm help, and the United States Department of Agriculture.

"Playin' right into their hands!" he complained. "A man ain't got no faith in a country that'll let a powerful group knock off the whole derned agricultural economy for their own interests!"

"Do you mean the Farm Bloc?" inquired Everhart, while Wesley, lost in thought, sat gazing at the fields.

The farmer tooted his horn four times as he barked four words: "you . . . dern . . . tootin' . . . right!"

By the time he dropped them off on the outskirts of Meriden, he and Bill were just warming up to their discussion of the Farm Security Administration and the National Farmers Union.

"G'bye, lads!" he called, waving a calloused hand. "Be careful, now." He drove off chuckling, tooting his horn in farewell.

"Nice old buck," commented Everhart.

Wesley looked around: "It's almost sundown; we gotta move."

They walked across a deserted traffic zone and stood in front of a lunchcart. Great elms drooped above them in sunset stillness, calmly exuding their day's warmth. A dog barked, breaking the quiet of the supper hour.

"Sleepy little place," nodded Everhart with a faint smile. "I wonder what it would be like to live in a town like this—digesting one's supper on the hammock facing the apple orchard, slapping off the mosquitoes, and retiring to the lullaby of a million crickets."

"Sounds right peaceful," smiled Wesley. "My hometown, Bennington, was a lot like this. I used to go swimmin' in a little mill pond not a half-mile back o' the house," his voice softening in recollection, "and when the moon came out, I used to sit on the little sand beach and smoke—keep the mosquiters off . . ."

"We'll have to go there someday," planned Bill with a cheerful grin. "Your family up there?"

Wesley frowned darkly and waved his hand: "Nah!"

"What do you mean?"

"When the old lady died," muttered Wesley with sullen reluctance, "the family broke up; we sold the house. Charley went to Boston and went in the saloon business with my uncle."

"Who's Charley?"

"The old man."

"What happened to the rest of the family?" Everhart pursued with quiet concern.

"Sisters married off, brothers beat it—one of them's in New Orleans, saw him in thirty-nine."

Everhart laid a hand on Wesley's shoulder: "The old homestead all gone, heh? An old story in American life, by George. It's the most beautiful and most heart-breaking story in American literature, from Dresser to Tom Wolfe—yes, you can't go home again . . ."

Wesley broke a twig in half and threw it away.

"I don't reckon you can, man," at length, he said, in a half whisper. "All depends where your home is . . . lose one, make another."

They were silent after that until a grocery truck picked them up. The grocer took them three miles up the road to a lonely crossroads lit by a streetlamp. In the near-darkness, they began to worry about getting to Hartford, fifteen miles or so to the north.

While Bill waited for a car to come along, Wesley foraged in a nearby orchard and returned with a handful of small green apples. "Don't eat them," he warned, "you'll be sick. Watch me pop that sign up ahead." Bill laughed as Wesley wound up elaborately and hurled the missiles against the sign.

"Good exercise," grunted Wesley. "I used to be a semi-pro baseball player . . . a pitcher . . . the Bennington Blues. Great game. Do you know where I played my last baseball game?"

"Where?" grinned Bill, adjusting his glasses.

Wesley threw the last apple and barely missed the target: "Hah!" he cursed. Turning and sinking his hands in his pockets he addressed Bill with a faint smile: "some seamen and me played a game of scrub in a field in Bombay. We had baseball equipment in the cargo for American soldiers and the Looey let us use it—gloves, balls, bats, all brand new."

A car was coming along the road.

"Give him the old number twelve," advised Wesley. "Watch!" He rotated his hand slowly, thumb outthrust. The auto roared past stubbornly.

"America . . . the beautiful," sang Wesley, "and crown thy good . . . with brotherhood . . . from sea to shining . . . seeeee!" His body was shaking with silent laughter.

Bill sat down on his suitcase and grinned. Up the road a faint light glowed in the window of a farmhouse. The air, heavy with all the accumulated heat of the day, the tang of heated foliage, stenches from a nearby swamp, the smell of the farmyard, and the cooling macadam of the road hung about them, a warm, sweet, voluptuous drape in the summer dusk.

"By George," burst Everhart, "if we don't get a ride we'll sleep right here in that orchard!"

Wesley lit up a cigarette he had found in his coat pocket: "It's been done," he offered. "But hell, man, we can't spend a whole night without butts."

"You smoke like a fiend."

"Here comes another car. Watch me get us a ride!"

Wesley succeeded; the car slowed to a halt abreast of them. They were in Hartford in thirty minutes, standing directly in front of the Public Library on Main Street. It was nine o'clock.

"Well!" said Bill, putting down his suitcase. "We've come halfway to Boston in six hours. Nine o'clock. Nine o'clock last night I didn't even know you, Wes!"

Wesley made no comment; he was watching people stroll by.

"Look what twenty-four hours and a moment of determination can do!" continued Bill, pushing his hat back. "I'm on my way . . . all of a sudden. Hell! I'm glad I did it. It's going to be a change. I call this life! Do you know, Wes, you're a pioneer in your own right."

Wesley stared at his companion curiously.

"I was wrong when I said the days of the pioneers were over, yes, even in my lectures. There's one on every street corner, by George. I've always been fascinated by pioneers and the pioneer spirit . . . when I was a kid, reading period pieces, French-Indian war sagas, Lincoln's life, Boone, Clark, Rogers . . . and when I grew older, I discovered the pioneer spirit in many writers, notably Americans. Change is the health of society. Or is it? I guess I'm a naturally restless person, that may explain it. . . ."

Wesley picked up Bill's suitcase. "Let's have a few cold beers," he proposed.

"Righto!"

"There's a place," noted Wesley, gesturing toward the other side of the street. "Let's mosey over."

While they crossed, Bill talked on: "I think I realize now why the pioneer spirit always guided me in my thinking—it's because he's free, Wes, free! He is like the skylark when contrasted to the settler, the man who plants his roots and leans back. The pioneer is free because he moves on and forgets to leave a trace. God!"

They entered a rowdy-looking barroom and occupied a booth with a sticky tabletop. Drinkers of all types sat ranged at the bar, old barflies, soldiers, broken-down hags, loud young men who gestured constantly at one another, and an occasional workingman still clad in his soiled workclothes.

A waitress brought them two large beers; and, leaning an indifferent hand on the back of the booth, she said: "Twenty dollars, darlings."

Wesley winked at her briefly while Bill threw two dimes on the table. She gave Wesley a hard, challenging look as she scooped up the coins: "honey," she told him huskily, "take care of them eyes."

"What's wrong with them?" demanded Wesley.

"They'll get you into trouble," she replied still watching him with heavy, malign ravishment. She backed away with a serious, brooding countenance, her eyes locked on Wesley's. He answered her eyes with the same challenging impudence, the same slow, sensual defiance, the bid of brute to brute.

"My God!" snickered Bill when she had left. "So this is Hartford! The rape of Wesley Martin!"

Wesley rubbed the side of his nose.

"Brother," he said quietly, "that's something that can kill a whole ship's crew in two weeks."

Everhart roared with laughter while Wesley drank his beer with a crafty smile.

Later, after a few beers, they ate pork chops in a lunch-cart on Main Street where Wesley bought two packages of Luckies and gave one of them to a vag who had begged for a cigarette.

"Where are we going to sleep?" Bill asked when they were back in the street. Wesley was picking his teeth with a toothpick.

"If this was New York," he said, "we could sleep in an all-night show or a subway. Hell, I dunno."

They roamed up and down Main Street, peering into bars and smoking. Finally, they grew restless; Wesley suggested they take in a late movie, but Everhart was dubious: "What are we going to eat with tomorrow?" he told Wesley.

"Who gives a shuck-all about tomorrow!" Wesley muttered scornfully. "Let's see a movie."

They went in. At midnight, they were back in the street; it was almost deserted. A few aircraft workers were returning from work in groups, talking in low, tired tones. A policeman teetered on his heels beside a cigar store.

"We'd better duck before we're pulled in," suggested Wesley. "Let's go see if we can find a place to sleep a few hours, before sunup."

"It's warm enough to sleep out," added Bill.

They walked East across the bridge and over to East Hartford. A dark, vacant lot offered plenty of thick matty grass, so they slumped down behind a clump of shrubs. Wesley was asleep in five minutes.

Everhart couldn't sleep for an hour. He lay on his back and watched the richly clustered stars high above; a cricket chirped not three feet away. The grass was damp, though he could feel its substratum of sunfed warmth. A coolness had crept into the night air; Bill pulled his collar up. He heard steps sounding down a nearby gravel path . . . a cop? Bill glanced over; he saw nothing in the darkness. A door opened, closed.

Well! Here he was sleeping in a backlot, a man with a post in a University, like so many other tramps. Wesley, there, sleeping as though nothing in the world mattered to him; one couldn't call him a tramp, could one? Who was this strange young man, very much a boy and yet very much a man? A seaman . . . yes, Everhart too would be a seaman.

Why?

Why had he done this? If his life in New York had seemed purposeless and foolish, then what could one call this life, this aimless wandering? If war had called Ulysses away from Syracuse, what had called Everhart away from New York?

Often he had told his classes about Fate, quoting devotedly from Emerson, from Shakespeare; he had spoken of Fate with the cheerful certainty that only a pedagogue could attain. That was his trouble, he had been a fearless pedagogue. And now? Certainly not a fearless man; he was full of fear, and why not? . . . he knew not what was coming. Would fear, the knowledge and the wisdom of fear, drive the pedantry from his foolish being?

What of Fate? Ah, she was a charming lady, Fate, see how she had woven her skin from New York to Hartford in a few brief hours, changed a man from a pedagogue to a trembling scholar, had made her day sunny and her night warm with the thrill and potency of mystery, had stolen to his side and for a moment of terrible glory, in the night, revealed to him her design of designs—that no man may know, but each may wait, wonder, and, according to the powers of his spirit, resist!

Everhart raised himself on his elbows . . . . the cricket stopped its song, fearful . . . . all the world slumbered in a massive hush. He could hear Wesley's slow breathing; above the stars nodded silently, nameless and far. "Me?" cried Wesley.

Everhart jumped nervously, his heart suddenly . . . pounding with fear. But Wesley was asleep—he had cried out in a dream.

Wesley was shaking his arm.

"Wake up, Bill, we're rollin'," he was saying in a husky morning voice.

It was still dark, but a few birds had begun to twitter a tiny alarum from the mist. Everhart rolled over and groaned: "What?"

"Wake up man, you ain't home?"

Everhart sat up rigidly, stupefied.

"By George," he growled, "you're right!"

Wesley was sitting on the grass, yawning and stretching his arms. The morning mist seeped into them with a raw, chill silence. "Let's move," repeated Wesley, "before we freeze to death."

They rose and walked off toward the street, not particularly inclined to talk to one another; an auto went by, leaving its rush of dust and gasoline fumes, growling off up the misty street like an ill-tempered old dog. Over the rooftops, a gray light was manifesting itself. It was a gloomy, unpleasant morning.

The two travelers had coffee in a lunch cart near the railroad tracks and scowled in unison when the counterman told them they looked as though they'd spend the night in a barn.

Once again in the street, the gray light had spread wide across the sky; they saw heavy clouds rushing in to darken the morning.

"Might rain," grunted Everhart.

They walked down the road and turned slowly as a car approached. It passed them swiftly, giving both a glimpse of a sleepy, surly face at the wheel. The road looked clean and ready for a new day in the dim morning light; it stretched up a hill and around a curve, beyond which they could make out a horizon of telephone poles, farms (winking small breakfast lights), and further beyond, rangy gray hills almost undiscernible in the mist. It smelled rain.

"Oh Christ!" yawned Wesley loudly. "I'll be glad when I can crawl into my berth!"

"Are you sure about that ship in Boston?"

"Yeah . . . The *Westminster*, transport-cargo, bound for Greenland; did you bring your birth certificate, man?"

Everhart slapped his wallet: "Right with me."

Wesley yawned again, pounding his breast as if to put a stop to his sleepiness. Everhart found himself wishing he were back home in his soft bed, with four hours yet to sleep before Sis's breakfast, while the milkman went by down on Claremont Avenue and a trolley roared past on sleepy Broadway.

A drop of rain shattered on his brow.

"We'd best get a ride right soon!" muttered Wesley turning to gaze down the deserted road.

They took shelter beneath a tree while the rain began to patter softly on the overhead leaves; a wet, steamy aroma rose in a humid wave.

"Rain, rain go away," Wesley sang softly, "come again another day . . ."

Ten minutes later, a big red truck picked them up. They smiled enthusiastically at the driver.

"How far you goin', pal?" asked Wesley.

"Boston!" roared the driver, and for the next hundred and twenty miles, while they traveled through wet fields along glistening roads, past steaming pastures and small towns, through a funeral [in] Worcester, down a splashing macadam highway leading directly toward Boston under lowering skies, the truckman said nothing further.

Everhart was startled from a nervous sleep when he heard Wesley's voice . . . . hours had passed swiftly.

"Boston, man!"

He opened his eyes; they were rolling along a narrow, cobblestoned street, flanked on each side with grim warehouses. It had stopped raining.

"How long have I been sleeping?" grinned Bill, rubbing his eyes while he held the spectacles on his lap.

"Dunno," answered Wesley, drawing from his perennial cigarette. The truck driver pulled to a lurching halt.

"Okay?" he shouted harshly.

Wesley nodded: "thanks a million, buddy. We'll be seeing you."

"So long, boys," he called. "See you again!"

Everhart jumped down from the high cab and stretched his legs luxuriously, waving his hand at the truck driver. Wesley stretched his arms slowly: "Eeyah! That was a long ride; I slept a bit myself."

They stood on a narrow sidewalk, which had already begun to dry after the brief morning rain. Heavy trucks piled past in the street, rumbling on the ancestral cobbles, and it wasn't until a group of them had gone, leaving the street momentarily deserted and clear of exhaust fumes, that Bill detected a clean sea smell in the air. Above, broken clouds scuttled across the luminous silver skies; a ray of warmth had begun to drop from the part of the sky where a vague dazzle hinted the position of the sun.

"I've been to Boston before," chatted Bill, "but never like this . . . this is the real Boston."

Wesley's face lit in a silent laugh: "I think you're talkin' through your hat again man! Let's start the day off with a beer on Scollay Square."

They walked on in high spirits.

Scollay Square was a short five minutes away. Its subway entrances, movie marquees, cut-rate stores, passport photo studios, lunchrooms, cheap jewelry stores and bars faced the busy traffic of the street with a vapid morning sullenness. Scores of sailors in Navy whites sauntered along the cluttered pavements, stopping to gaze at cheap store fronts and theater signs.

Wesley lead Bill to a passport photo studio where an old man charged them a dollar for two small photos.

"They're for your seaman's papers," explained Wesley. "How much money does that leave you?"

"A quarter," Everhart grinned sheepishly.

"Two beers and a cigar; let's go," Wesley said, rubbing his hands. "I'll borrow a fin from a seaman."

Everhart looked at his pictures: "Don't you think I look like a tough seadog here?"

"Hell man, yes!" cried Wesley.

In the bar they drank a bracing glass of cold beer and talked about Polly, Day, Ginger and Eve.

"Nice bunch of kids," said Wesley slowly.

Everhart gazed thoughtfully at the bartap: "I'm wondering how long Polly waited for us last night. I'll bet this is the first time Madame Butterfly was ever stood up!" he added with a grin. "Polly's quite the belle around Columbia, you know." It sounded strange to say "Columbia" . . . how far away was it now?

"I didn't mean to play a wood on her," said Wesley at length. "But hell, when you're on the move, you're on the move! I'll see her some other time."

"Won't George Day be surprised when he learns I've gone and wasn't fooling about joining the Merchant Marine!" laughed Bill. "I left on the spur of the moment. It'll be the talk of the place."

"What's Eve gonna say?" asked Wesley.

"Oh I don't know; I never was very serious with Eve, anyway. We've had a lot of great times together, parties and all that, but we were just good friends. I haven't been serious over a girl since I was in my teens."

A sailor behind them slid a nickel into the big music box and danced slowly across the floor as Bing Crosby sang "Please Don't Take My Sunshine Away."

"Pop!" shouted the young sailor, addressing the bartender, "It's a great man's Navy!"

"Keep it that way," answered the older man. "It was in my day. Come on over here till I set you up a drink—what'll you have? Take your choice!"

"Pop!" bellowed the sailor flopping on a stool, "I'm gonna set up you to a drink, you bein' an old Navy man yerself." He produced a dark brown bottle from his hip pocket. "Jamaica Rum!" he announced proudly.

"All right," said the bartender, "you give me a swallow o' that Rum and I'll set you up a drink that'll make your eyes pop."

"Impossible," muttered the sailor, turning to Wesley. "Am I right?"

"Right!" said Wesley.

The sailor handed his bottle over to Wesley: "Try some o' that Jamaica Rum, buddy; try it."

Wesley nodded and proceeded to wash down a long draught; recapping the bottle he handed it back without comment.

"Well?" asked the sailor.

"Right!" snapped Wesley.

The sailor turned, brandishing the bottle: "Right, he says . . . damn right it's right. This is Jamaica Rum, imported . . . Johnny's own whoopee water!"

When Bill and Wesley finished their beers, they walked out in silence; at the door Wesley turned as the sailor called him: "Right, feller?"

Wesley pointed his forefinger toward the sailor.

"Right!" he shouted, winking an eye.

"Right, he says!" sang the sailor once more flourishing his bottle.

"Well! We're in Boston," beamed Bill when they were back on the street. "What's on the docket?"

"First thing to do," said Wesley, leading his companion across the street, "is to mosey over to the Union Hall and check up on the *Westminster* . . . we might get a berth right off."

They walked down Hanover Street, with its cheap shoe stores and bauble shops, and turned left at Portland Street, a battered door, bearing the inscription "National

Maritime Union," lead up a flight of creaking steps into a wide, rambling hall. Grimy windows at each end served to allow a gray light from outside to creep inward a gloomy, half-hearted illumination which outlined the bare, unfurnished immensity of the room. Only a few benches and folding chairs had been pushed against the walls, and these were now occupied by seamen who sat talking in low tones: they were dressed in various civilian clothing, but Everhart instantly recognized them as sea-men . . . there, in the dismal gloom of their musty-smelling shipping headquarters, these men sat, each with the patience and passive quiet of men who know they are going back to sea, some smoking pipes, others calmly perusing the "Pilot," official N.M.U publication, others dozing on the benches, and all possessed of the serene waiting wisdom of a Wesley Martin.

"Wait here," said Wesley, shuffling off toward the partitioned office across the broad plank floor. "I'll be right back." Everhart sat on the suitcase, peering.

"Hey Martin!" howled a greeting voice from the folding chairs. "Martin you old crum!" A seaman was running across the hall toward Wesley, whooping with delight in his discovery. The echoing cries failed to disturb the peace of the other seamen, though, indeed; they glanced briefly and curiously toward the noisy reunion.

Wesley was astounded.

"Jesus!" he cried. "Nick Meade!"

Meade fairly collapsed into Wesley, almost knocking him over in his zeal to come to grips in a playful, bearish embrace; they pounded each other enthusiastically, and at one point Meade went so far as to push Wesley's chin gently with his fist, calling him as he did so every conceivable name he could think of; Wesley, for his part, manifested his delight by punching his comrade squarely in the stomach and howling a vile epithet as he did so. They whooped it up raucously for at least a half a minute while Everhart grinned appreciatively from his suitcase.

Then Meade asked a question in a low tone, hand on Wesley's shoulder; the latter answered confidentially, to which Meade roared once more and began anew to pummel Wesley, who turned away, his thin frame shaking with soundless laughter. Presently, they made their way toward the office, exchanging news with the breathless rapidity of good friends who meet after a separation of years.

"Shipping out?" raced Meade.

"Yeah."

"Let's see Harry about a double berth."

"Make it three, I've got a mate with me."

"Come on! The *Westminster*'s in port; she's taking on 'most a full crew."

"I know."

"You old son of a bitch!" cried Meade, unable to control his joy at the chance meeting. "I haven't seen you since forty," kicking Wesley in the pants, "when we got canned in Trinidad!"

"For startin' that riot!" remembered Wesley, kicking back playfully while Meade dodged aside. "You friggin' communist, don't start. Kickin' me again . . . I remember the time you got drunk aboard ship and went around kickin' everybody till that big Bosun1 pinned your ears back!"

They howled their way into the inner office where a sour faced Union man looked up blandly from his papers.

"Act like seamen, will you?" he growled.

"Hangover Harry," informed Meade. "He uses up all the dues money to get drunk. Look at that face will you?"

"All right Meade," admonished Harry. "What are you looking for, I'm busy . . ."

They made arrangements to be on hand and near the office door that afternoon when the official ship calls from the *S.S. Westminster* would be posted, although Harry warned them those first come would be first served. "Two-thirty sharp," he grunted. "If you're not here, you don't get the jobs."

Wesley introduced Meade to Everhart and they all went around the corner for a quick beer. Meade was a talkative, intelligent young man in his late twenties who stroked an exquisite brown moustache with voluptuous afterthought as he rambled on, a faint twinkle in the bland blue eyes, walking in a quickstepping glide that wove between pedestrians as though they were not there. On the way to the bar on Hanover Street, he shouted at least three insults to various passersby who amused his carefree fancy.

At the bar, he and Wesley reminisced noisily over their past experiences together, all of which Everhart drank in with polite interest. Some other seamen hailed them from a corner booth, so they all carried their beers over, and an uproar of reunion ensued. Wesley seemed to know them all.

But a half hour later, Wesley rose and told Meade to meet him in the Union Hall at two thirty; and with this, he and Everhart left the bar and turned their steps toward Atlantic Avenue.

"Now for your seaman's paper," he said to Bill.

Atlantic Avenue was almost impossible to cross, so heavy was the rush of traffic, but once they had regained the other side and stood near a pier, Bill's breast pounded as he saw, docked not a hundred feet away, a great gray freighter, its slanting hull striped with rust, a thin stream of water arching from its scuppers, and the mighty bow standing high above the roof of the wharf shed.

"Is that it?" he cried.

"No, she's at Pier Six."

They walked toward the Maritime Commission, the air heavy with the rotting stench of stockpiles, oily-waters, fish, and hemp. Dreary marine equipment stores faced the street, show windows cluttered with blue peacoats, dungarees, naval officers' uniforms, small compasses, knives, oilers' caps, seamen's wallets, and all manner of paraphernalia for the men of the sea.

The Maritime Commission occupied one floor of a large building that faced the harbor. While a pipe-smoking old man was busy preparing his papers, Everhart could see beyond the nearby wharves and railroad yards, a bilious stretch of sea spanning toward the narrows, where two lighthouses stood like gate posts to a dim Atlantic. A seagull swerved past the window.

An energetic little man fingerprinted him in the next room, cigarette in mouth almost suffocating him as he pressed Bill's inky fingers on the papers and on a duplicate.

"Now go down to the Post Office building," panted the little man when he had finished, "and get your passport certificate. Then you'll be all set."

Wesley was leaning against the wall smoking when Bill left the fingerprinting room with papers all intact.

"Passport certificate next I guess," Bill told Wesley, nodding toward the room.

"Right!"

They went to the Post Office building on Milk Street where Bill filled out an application for his passport and was handed a certificate for his first foreign voyage; Wesley, who had borrowed five dollars from Nick Meade, paid Bill's fee.

"Now I'm finished I hope?" laughed Bill when they were back in the street.

"That's all."

"Next thing is to get our berths on the *Westminster*. Am I correct?"

"Right."

"Well," smiled Bill, slapping his papers, "I'm in the merchant marine."

At two-thirty that afternoon, Wesley, Bill, Nick Meade and seven other seamen landed jobs on the S.S. Westminster. They walked from the Union Hall down to Pier Six in high spirits, passing through the torturous weave of Boston's waterfront streets, crossing Atlantic Avenue and the Mystic river drawbridge, and finally coming to a halt along the Great Northern Avenue docks. Silently they gazed at the S.S. Westminster, looming on their left, her monstrous gray mass squatting broadly in the slip, very much, to Everhart's astonished eyes, like an old bath-tub.

CHAPTER FIVE

"She's what we call a medium sized transport-cargo ship," a seaman had told Everhart as they all marched down the huge shed toward the gang plank, waving greetings to the longshoremen who were busy hauling the cargo aboard, rolling oil barrels down the hold, swinging great loads of lumber below decks with the massive arm of a boom. "She does fifteen knots full steam, cruises at twelve. Not much speed—but she can weather plenty."

And when they had shown their job slips to the guard at the gang plank and begun to mount the sagging boards, Bill had felt a strange stirring in the pit of his guts—he was boarding a ship for the first time in his life! A ship, a great proud bark back from homeless seas and bound for others perhaps stranger and darker than any it had ever wandered to . . . and he was going along!

Bill was lying in his bunk, remembering these strange sensations he had felt in the afternoon. It was now evening.

From his position in an upper berth, he could see the dark wall of the dock shed through an open porthole. It was a hot breathless night. The focastle he had been assigned to was partitioned off from another by a plate of white painted, riveted steel, aft to port. Two brilliant light bulbs illuminated the small room from a steel overhead. There were two double berths, upper and lower, and a small sink; four lockers, two battered folding chairs, and a three-legged stool completed the furnishings of this bare steel chamber.

Bill glanced over at the other seaman who had been assigned to the same quarters. He was sleeping, his puckish young features calm in slumber. He couldn't be over eighteen years old, Bill reflected. Probably had been going to sea for years despite everything.

Bill pulled the job slip from his wallet and mulled over the writing: "William Everhart, ordinary seaman, *S.S. Westminster*, deck crew mess boy." Messboy! . . . William Everhart, A.B., M.A., assistant professor of English and American Literature at Columbia University . . . a mess boy! Surely, this would be a lesson in humility, he chuckled, even though he had never gone through life under the pretext that he was anything but humble, at least, a humble young pedant.

He lay back on the pillow and realized these were his first moments of solitary deliberation since making his rash decision to get away from the thoughtless futility of his past life. It had been a good life, he ruminated, a life possessing at least a minimum of service and security. But he wasn't sorry he had made this decision; it would be a change, as he'd so often repeated to Wesley, a change regardless of everything. And the money was good in the merchant marine, the companies were not reluctant to reward the seamen for their labor and courage; money of that amount would certainly be welcomed at home, especially now with the old man's need for medical care. It would be a relief to pay for his operation and perhaps soften his rancor against a household that had certainly done him little justice. In his absorption for his work and the insistent demands of a highly paced social life, Bill admitted to himself, as he had often done, he had not proved an attentive son; there were such distances between a father and his son, a whole generation of differences in temperament, tastes, views, habits: yet the old man, sitting in that old chair with his pipe, listening to an ancestral radio while the new one boomed its sleek, modern power from the living room, was he not fundamentally the very meaning and core of Bill Everhart, the creator of all that Bill Everhart had been given to work with? And what right, Bill now demanded angrily, had his sister and brother-in-law to neglect him so spiritually? What if he were a lamenting old man?

Slowly, now, Everhart began to realize why life had seemed so senseless, so fraught with fully lack of real purpose in New York, in the haste and oration of his teaching days—he had never paused to take hold of anything, let alone the lonely heart of an old father, not even the idealisms with which he had begun life as a seventeen-year-old spokesman for the working class movement on Columbus Circle Saturday afternoons. All these he had lost, by virtue of a sensitivity too fragile for everyday disillusionment . . . his father's complaints, the jeers of the Red baiters and the living, breathing social apathy that supported their jeers in phlegmatic silence. A few shocks from the erratic fuse box of life, and Everhart had thrown up his hands and turned to a life of academic isolation. Yet, in the realms of this academic isolation, wasn't there sufficient indication that all things pass and turn to dust? What was that sonnet where Shakespeare spoke sonorously of time "rooting out the work of masonry?"1 Is a man to be timeless and patient, or is he to be a pawn of time? What did it avail a man to plant roots deep into a society by all means foolish and Protean?

Yet, Bill now admitted with reluctance, even Wesley Martin had set himself a purpose, and this purpose was the ideal of life—life at sea—a Thoreau before the mast.

Conviction had lead Wesley to the sea; confusion had lead Everhart to the sea.

A confused intellectual, Everhart, the oldest weed in society; beyond that, an intelligent modern minus the social conscience of that class. Further, a son without a conscience—a lover without a wife! A prophet without confidence, a teacher of men without wisdom, a sorry mess of man thereat!

Well, things would be different from now on . . . a change of life might give him the proper perspective. Surely, it had not been folly to take a vacation from his bookish, bearish life, as another side of his nature might deny! What wrong was there in treating his own life, within the bounds of moral conscience, as he chose and as he freely wished? Youth was still his, the world might yet open its portals as it had done that night at Carnegie Hall in 1927 when he first heard the opening bars of Brahms' first symphony! Yes! As it opened its doors for him so many times in his teens and closed them firmly, as though a stern and hostile master were its doorman, during his enraged twenties.

Now he was thirty-two years old and it suddenly occurred to him that he had been a fool, yes, even though a lovable fool, the notorious "short pants" with the erudite theories and the pasty pallor of a teacher of life . . . and not a liver of life. Wasn't it Thomas Wolfe who had struck a brief spark in him at twenty-six and filled him with new love for life until it slowly dawned on him that Tom Wolfe—as his colleagues agreed in delighted unison—was a hopeless romanticist? What of it? What if triumph were Wolfe's only purpose? . . . if life was essentially a struggle, then why not struggle toward triumph, why not, in that case, achieve triumph! Wolfe had failed to add to whom triumph was liege . . . and that, problem though it was, could surely be solved, solved in the very spirit of his cry for triumph. Wolfe had sounded the old cry of a new world. Wars come, wars go! Elated Bill to himself, this cry is an insurgence against the forces of evil, which creeps in the shape of submission to evil, this cry is a denial of the not-good and a plea for the good. Would he, then, William Everhart plunge his whole being into a new world? Would he love? Would he labor? Would he, by God, fight?

Bill sat up and grinned sheepishly.

"By George," he mumbled aloud, "I might at that!"

"Might what?" asked the other seaman, who was awake and sitting up with his legs dangling over the bunk rail.

Bill turned a bashful face, laughing.

"Oh I was only muttering to myself."

The young seaman said nothing. After a strained pause, he at length spoke up.

"This your first trip?"

"Yes."

"What the hell time is it?" asked the youth.

"About nine o'clock."

There was another silence. Bill felt he had better explain his strange behavior before his focastle mate should take him for a madman, but he couldn't conceive of any explanation. The young seaman apparently overlooked the incident, for he wanted to know why in hell they weren't ashore getting drunk.

Everhart explained that he was waiting to go out with two other seamen in a half-hour.

"Well, I'll be in the mess. Pick me up on the way out," directed the youth. "My name's Eathington."

"All right, we'll do that; my name's Everhart."

The youngster shuffled off lazily: "Glad t' meetcha," he said, and was gone.

Bill vaulted down from his bunk and went to the sink for a drink of water. He leaned over and thrust his head [out] of the porthole, peering aft along the shed wall. The harbor was still and dark, except for a cluster of lights far across where a great drydock was illumined for its night shift. Two small lights, a red and a blue one, chased one another calmly across the dark face of the bay, the sound of the launch's motor puttering quietly. From the direction of dimmed-out Boston came a deep prolonged sigh of activity.

"By God!" Bill told himself, "I haven't felt like this in a long time. If I'm going to fight for this new world, where better than on a merchant ship laden with fighting cargoes? And if I'm going to lay my plans for a new life, where better to devise them than at sea—a vacation from life, to return brown and rugged and spiritually equipped for all its damned devious tricks!" He paced the focastle silently.

"And when I get back," he thought, "I'll keep my eyes open . . . if there's anything insincere afoot in this war, I'll smell it out, by George, and I'll fight it! I used to have ideas a long time ago—I had spark: we'll see what happens. I'm ready for anything . . . good Christ, I don't believe I've been as downright foolish as this in a long time, but it's fun, it's new, and Goddamn it, it's refreshing."

Bill stopped in the middle of the room and appraised it curiously, adjusting his spectacles; "A ship, by George! I wonder when we sail . . ."

Laughing voices broke his reverie; it was Nick Meade and Wesley coming down the gangway.

"All set, man?" cried Wesley. "Let's go out and drink some of my old man's whiskey!"

"All set," said Bill. "I'm just sitting around trying to accustom myself to the fact I'm on a ship . . ."

They went down the gangway and into the mess hall. A group of soldiers sat drinking coffee at one of the long tables.

"Who are they?" asked Bill curiously.

"Gun crew," raced Meade.

Young Eathington was sitting alone with a cup of coffee. Bill waved at him: "Coming?" he shouted, adding quietly to Wesley: "He's in my focastle; mind if he comes along with us?"

Wesley waved his hand; "Free booze! More the merrier."

They passed through the galley, with its aluminum cauldrons, hanging pots and pans, a massive range and a long pantry counter. One big cook stood peering into a cauldron with a corn cob pipe clamped in his teeth; he was a big colored man, and as he stood ruminating over his steaming soup, his basso voice hummed a strange melody.

"Hey Glory!" howled Nick Meade at the giant cook. "Come on out and get drunk."

Glory turned and removed the pipe from his mouth. "It's a hipe!" he commented in a rumbling, moaning voice. "You boys goin' out thar in git boozed."

Young Eathington smiled puckishly: "What the hell d'you think, Glory? We gotta drown down the taste of your lousy soup!"

Glory's eyes widened in simulated astonishment.

"It's a hipe!" he boomed. "A lowdown hipe! Them little chillun are goin' out than in git boozed."

As they laughed their way down the midships gangway, they could hear Glory resume his humming.

"Where's everybody on this ship?" asked Bill. "It's deserted."

"They're all out drinking," answered Meade. "Glory's probably the only one on board now. You'll see them all tomorrow morning at breakfast."

"Saturday night," added Eathington.

They were descending the gangplank.

"Hear what that big boy was singing?" Wesley said, "Them's way down blues. Heard that singing in Virginia long time ago on a construction job. Way down blues, man."

"Where we goin'?" asked Eathington, tilting his oiler's cap at a jaunty angle.

"My old man's saloon in the South End."

"Free booze?" added Everhart, adjusting his glasses with a grin.

"Free booze?" howled Eathington, "C'mon, I'm not complainin' . . . I blew my last pay in a Charlestown poolroom."

In the street, they strode rapidly toward Atlantic Avenue. Nick Meade, who had signed on as an oiler, asked Eathington if he too had an engine room job.

"No; I'm on as a scullion; signed on yesterday; couldn't get anythin' better."

"Then what the hell are you wearing an oiler's cap for?" asked Meade.

The kid grinned wryly: "Just for the hell of it!"

Wesley's face lit up with delight: "Give me that hat!" he growled "I'm gonna throw the damn thing in the drink!" He advanced toward Eathington, but the kid broke into a run down the street laughing; Wesley was after him like a deer. Presently, Wesley was back wearing the cap, smiling wickedly.

"How do I look?" he asked.

They took a subway to the South End and went over to Charley Martin's "Tavern." It was, actually, one of the cheapest saloons Everhart had ever been privileged to enter. The planked floors were covered with sawdust and innumerable spittoons; several drunkards sprawled over their cups in the booths, and it took some time before

Everhart grew accustomed to the fact that one of them was a woman with legs like sticks.

Behind the bar, tuning the radio, was a man in a bartender's apron who looked very much like Wesley, except for his white hair and heavy jowls.

"There's the old buck," said Wesley, shuffling toward the bar. His father turned and saw him.

It was a very simple greeting: the older man raised his two hands and opened his mouth in a quiet, happy gesture of surprise. Then he advanced toward the edge of the bar, and still maintaining his surprise, he proffered one of his thin hands to his son. Wesley clasped it firmly and they shook hands.

"Well, well, well . . ." greeted Mr. Martin gravely.

"Howdy, Charley," said Wesley with a thin smile.

"Well, well, well . . ." repeated the silver haired, slim man, still clasping his son's hand and gazing at him with mixed gravity and concern. "Where have you been?"

"All over," answered Wesley.

"All over, hey?" echoed the father, still holding Wesley's hand. Then he turned slowly toward a group of men who sat at the bar watching the incident with proud smiles. "Boys," announced the father, "meet the kid. Drinks are on me."

As the father turned sternly to his bottles, Wesley had to shake hands with a half dozen grinning barflies.

Mr. Martin ranged glasses all along the bar with the slow flourish of a man who is performing a ritual of deep significance. Bill, Meade, and Eathington took seats beside Wesley. When the glasses had all been filled with Scotch, Mr. Martin poured himself a stiff portion in a water glass and turned slowly to face the entire gathering. A deep silence reigned.

"To the kid," toasted Mr. Martin, glass aloft.

They all drank without a word, including Wesley. When that was done, the night was on for Wesley and his shipmates, for the first thing the old man did was to refill their glasses.

"Drink up!" he commanded. "Wash the other one down!" They did.

Eathington went to the nickelodeon and played a Beatrice Kay recording.

"My old man was in show business," he shouted to the room in general; and to prove this he began to shuffle sideways across the barroom floor, cap in one hand and the other palm up in a vaudeville attitude that convulsed Everhart into a fit of laughter; Nick was bored. Wesley, for his part, was content to refill his glass from the quart bottle his father had left standing before them.

Fifteen minutes of this, and Everhart was well on his way to being drunk; every time he would drain his glass, Wesley would refill it gravely. Meade had lapsed into a reverie, but after a long stretch of that, he looked up and spoke to Everhart, stroking his moustache in sensual abstraction: "Wes tells me this is your first trip, Everhart."

"Yes, it is," admitted Bill apologetically.

"What were you doing?"

"Teaching at Columbia University, an assistant . . ."

"Columbia!" exclaimed Meade.

"Yes."

"I was kicked out of Columbia in thirty-five," laughed Meade. "My freshman year!"

"You?" said Bill. "Thirty-five? I was working for my master's degree then; that probably explains why I didn't know you."

Nick fingered his moustache and pulled at its ends thoughtfully.

"Why were you thrown out?" pursued Bill.

"Oh," said Nick flippantly, waving his hand, "I only went there with the express purpose of joining the students' Union. I was kicked out inside of a month."

"What for?" laughed Bill.

"I believe they said it was because I was a dangerous radical, inciting to riot and so forth."

Mr. Martin was standing in front of them.

"All set, boys?" he asked solemnly.

"That we are; Mr. Martin," smiled Bill. Mr. Martin reached a hand over and punched Wesley playfully. Wesley smiled faintly, very much the bashful son.

"Got enough to drink?" growled the father, his bushy white eyebrows drawn together in a sober, serious glare.

"Yup," answered Wesley with modest satisfaction.

The old man glared fixedly at Wesley for a space of seconds and then turned back to his work with ponderous solemnity.

Everhart had found a new comrade; he turned to Nick Meade enthusiastically and wanted to know all about his expulsion from Columbia.

Nick shrugged nonchalantly: "Not much to tell. I was simply bounced. I got myself a job downtown in a drugstore, down on East Tenth Street. When I found out the other employees weren't organized, I took a few of them up to a Union a couple of blocks away. When the manager refused to recognize our right of union, we sat down; he hired others so the next morning we picketed up and down. You should have seen him howl!"

"Did he give in?"

"He had to, the old crum."

"What'd you do after that?"

"Have another drink," offered Wesley to both of them, filling their glasses. When they went back to their conversation, Mr. Martin returned and began talking softly to Wesley in what seemed to Everhart a disclosure of a confidential nature.

"I hooked up with a couple of the boys," resumed Nick, lighting up a cigarette. "One night we decided to go to Spain, so off we went. We joined up with the Abe Lincoln International Brigade there. Three months later I was wounded outside of Barcelona, but you'd be surprised where. The nurse . . ."

"You fought for the Loyalists!" burst Everhart incredulously.

"Yeah"—caressing his moustache.

"Let me shake your hand on that, Meade," said Bill holding out his hand admiringly.

"Thanks," said Nick laconically.

"I wish I'd have done the same," raced Bill. "It was a rotten deal for the Spanish people, doublecrossed from every direction . . ."

"Rotten deal?" echoed Nick with a scoff. "It was worse than that, especially in the light of the way the whole satisfied world took it! There was Spain bleeding and the rest of the world did nothing; I got back to America all in one piece expecting to hear fireworks, and what did I see? I swear, some Americans didn't even know there'd been a war."

Everhart maintained a nodding silence.

"Those foul Fascists had all the time in the world to gird up, and who can deny it today? Franco took Spain and nobody raised a finger in protest. And how many of my buddies were killed for nothing? It wasn't nothing then, we were fighting Fascists and that was all right; but now that it's all over, and we look back on it, we all feel like a bunch of suckers. We were betrayed by everyone who could have helped us; including Leon Blum. But don't think for a moment that any of us have thrown up the towel—the more we get skunked, betrayed, and knifed in the back, I tell you, the more we'll come back fighting, and some day soon, we're going to do the dishing out . . . and the Spanish Loyalists as well."

Nick stroked his moustache bitterly: "My buddie's dishing it out right now," he said at length. "I wish to hell I were with him . . ."

"Where is he?"

"He's fighting with the Red Army. After we stole through Franco's lines we crossed the Pyrenees over to France. We knocked around Paris until they picked us up and deported us. From there we went to Moscow. When I left, he stayed behind; Goddamn it, I should have stayed too!"

"Why didn't you?"

"I met an American girl up there and shacked up with her; she was selling magazines for the Soviet. We came back to New York and holed up in Greenwich Village, and we've been living there since—got married three months ago—I've been in the Merchant Marine for three years now."

Everhart adjusted his glasses: "What's going to be your next move? Fighting French?"

"This is my next move—the merchant marine. We carry goods to our allies, don't we? We're fighting Fascism just as much as the soldier or sailor."

"True," agreed Everhart proudly.

"Of course it's true," spat Nick savagely.

"What are you going to do after the war?" pursued Bill.

"Après la guerre?" mused Nick sadly. "There'll still be a hell of a lot to fight for. I'm going back to Europe. France maybe. Watch our smoke . . ."

"Well, not to be personal, but what do you intend to do with your life in general?" asked Bill nervously.

Nick look at him blandly.

"Fight for the rights of man," he said quickly. "What else can one live for?"

Everhart found himself nodding slowly. Nick's blue, searching eyes were on him, eyes, Everhart thought, of the accusing masses, eyes that stirred him slowly to speak his mind by virtue of their calm challenge.

"Well," he began, "I hope you won't think I'm an old line fool . . . but when I was a kid, seventeen to be exact, I made speeches on Columbus Circle . . . I stood there and spoke to them out of my heart, young and immature and sentimental though it was, and they didn't hear me! You know that as well as I do. They're so ignorant, and in their ignorance, they are so pathetic, so helpless! When the Redbaiters hissed, they smiled at my plight . . ."

"The old story," interrupted Nick. "That sort of thing won't get us anywhere, you know that! You were doing more harm than good . . ."

"I know that, of course, but you know how it is when you're young . . ."

Nick grinned: "They had my picture all over the hometown front page at sixteen, the scandal of the community, the town radical—and guess what?"

"What?"

"My old lady was pleased! She used to be a hellcat herself, suffragette and all that . . ."

They laughed briefly, and Everhart resumed: "Well, at nineteen I gave it all up, disillusioned beyond recall. I went around there for awhile snapping at everyone who spoke to me. And slowly I sank all my being into my English studies; I deliberately avoided social studies. As you can imagine, the years went by—my mother died—and whatever social conscience I had in the beginning left me altogether. Like Rhett Butler, I frankly didn't give a damn . . . I ate up literature like a hog—especially Shakespeare, Donne, Milton, Chaucer, Keats, and the rest—and left a brilliant enough record to win me an assistant professorship in the university. Whatever social protest I came across in my lectures I treated from a purely objective point of view; in the reading and discussion of Dos Passos a few summers ago, I drew from his works simply from a literary standpoint. By George, where I started by deliberately avoiding Socialism I believe I wound up not particularly interested anyway. Insofar as I was in the university, living a gay enough though fruitless life, I didn't find the need to bother." Nick was silent.

"But I'll tell you something, those years taught me one lesson, and that was not to trust a lot of things. I always believed in the working class movement, even though I allowed it to slip my mind, but I know now what I didn't believe in all those years, with more unconscious rancor that with conscious hate." Bill peered eagerly.

"What was that?" asked Nick with cold suspicion.

"Politics for one thing, sheer politics. Politicians survive only if they make certain concessions; if they don't they go out of office. Thus, idealist or not, a politician is always faced with a vexing choice, sooner or later, between justice and survival. This will inevitably serve to mar his ideals, won't it?"

"That sounds natural; what else?"

"A dependence on group . . . I mistrust that, first because it means bending one's mind to a dogmatic group-will. When I say this, I refer not to an economic group where, to my mind, sharing and sharing alike is only natural, and inevitable too. I mean a spiritual group . . . there should be no such thing as a spiritual group; each man to his own spirit, Meade, each man to his own soul."

"What are you telling me this for?" Nick snapped.

"Because the day may come when the materialistic war you fight on the forces of Fascism and reaction will be won by you and yours—and me, by George. And when that day arrives, when the sharing class will rule, when the rights of man become obvious to all mankind, what will you be left with? Your equal share of the necessities of life?"

Nick's eyes flashed: "You poor dope! Do you mean to tell me a war against Fascism is a purely materializing one, as you say? A war against an ideology that has burned the books, has conceived a false hierarchy of the human races, has confused human kindness with weakness, has stamped upon all the accumulated cultures of Europe and substituted them with a cult of brutality inconceivable beyond . . ."

"Hold on!" laughed Bill, who, though astonished at Meade's unsuspected erudition, had nonetheless a point to make and would cling to it. "You're not telling me a thing. I want you to pause and think: erase the factor of Fascism, because it doesn't figure in our argument. Fascism is a freak, a perversion, a monster if you wish, that must be destroyed, and will be destroyed. But once that is done, our problems won't be solved; even if we write a satisfactory peace, a peace for the common man, the problem won't be solved. A world where men live in co-operative security is a world where there is no hunger, no want, no fear, and so forth. Men will *share* . . . I'm taking a long-range view of the whole thing . . . men will live in a world of economic equality. But the spirit will still be vexed; you seem to think it won't. Men will still deceive one another, cheat, run away with the other man's wife, rob, murder, rape . . ."

"Oh," cried Nick mincingly "you're one of those so-called students of human nature." He turned away.

"Wait! I'm not the retrogressive voice sounding from the pages of the Old Testament. I, too, like you, will deny human frailty as long as I live—will try to cure human nature in the tradition of the Progressive movement. But I don't see a quick and easy way out; I think anti-Fascists live under that delusion. They point to fascism as all of evil, they point to every home grown Fascist by nature as all of evil. They think that by destroying Fascism, they destroy all evil in the world today, where, I believe, they only destroy what may be the last grand concerted evil. When that is done, disorganized individual evil will still be with us . . ."

"Truisms!" spat Nick. "A child would know that!"

"And I more than anyone else, if you will pardon my insufferable vanity . . . but I brought up the subject for one single reason, to point out that being simply anti-Fascist is not enough. You've got to go beyond anti-Fascism, you've got to be more meticulous in your search for a life's purpose."

"It's purpose enough for anyone in these times," countered Nick. "You don't know Fascists like I do, I'm afraid."

"You say," persisted Bill swiftly, "you live for the rights of man; aren't you supposed to live for life itself? Are the rights of man . . . life?"

"They are to me," was the icy rejoinder.

"And only a part of life to me," smiled Bill, "—an important part of life, but not all of life."

"Do you know what you are?" posed Nick, a good deal annoyed. "you're one of these befuddled, semi-aristocratic 'intellectuals' who will rave at discussion tables while men starve outside . . ."

"I would not, and incidentally we were assuming regimented injustice had ceased."

At that, Nick stared squarely into Bill's eyes.

"All right Professor, let's say it has," Nick proposed.

"What are you left with besides economic . . ."

"I'm left with a world," interrupted Nick, "where all your blasted theories of this and that can at least be put into action without suppression!"

"Didn't I say Fascism was our more immediate problem?" pressed Bill.

"You did. So what?"

"Then, this later problem, can it be solved with a sword of righteousness or by the spirit itself?"

"This later problem, as you call it, is not important at this particular moment," Nick rejoined. "Your profound theories don't arrest me in the least . . ."

"Which makes you an iconoclast!" smiled Bill.

"All right, and which makes you a new type of reactionary . . . and a slacker; here, let's drink up the Scotch and argue some other time." Nick was disgusted.

Bill raised his glass to him: "Well, at least you'll have someone to argue with on this trip. Let's you and I drink to Socialism!"

Nick turned a weary, lidded eye on Bill: "Please don't be a fool . . . I hate Socialists more than I do Capitalists."

Bill smiled craftily and started to sing: "Arise ye prisoners of starvation, a better world's in birth, for justice thunders . . ."

"That's enough!" interrupted Nick impatiently.

"What's the matter?"

"Let's drink our toasts; but I don't want to sing the *International* in a tavern—it's a drunken insult."

Bill touched Nick's glass. "Sorry—here's to."

During this lengthy argument, Wesley had been drinking steadily; almost, it would seem, with a deliberate desire to become intoxicated. Eathington, in the meantime, had found himself someone to talk to in a back booth.

While Everhart and Meade talked on, Mr. Martin returned to Wesley and again spoke to him privately in a low tone.

"She just got in—she says she's comin' right over," said the old man, gazing anxiously at his son. Both father and son stared fixedly at one another, with the same immobile intensity Everhart had first noticed in Wesley when they had exchanged a long glance in the Broadway bar.

They held their gaze and said nothing for many seconds. Then Wesley shrugged.

"None o' my doin', son," growled Mr. Martin. "She located me an' told me if you ever came to call her up. She's been in that hotel for two months waitin' for you to pop up. None o' my doin'."

Wesley refilled his glass: "I know it ain't."

The old man glared heavily at his son, wiping the bar briefly with a towel. It was not ten thirty; the room had filled up considerably, keeping the waitress busy serving drinks from the bar to the booths.

"Well, it won't do no harm," added Mr. Martin. "I got some work to do." He went back to his work solemnly. By this time, a young assistant bartender had arrived, and he now dashed furiously from bottle to mixer, glass to tap as the orders mounted. Mr. Martin, though he moved slowly, succeeded in mixing more drinks and pouring more beers, all of which set swifter pace for the harassed young helper. Music from the nickelodeon played incessantly while the screen door slammed time and again as patrons arrived or

left. The air was close and sticky, though the ceiling fans
succeeded in blowing a beery breeze about.

Wesley filled Bill's and Nick's glasses with a morose silence while they launched enthusiastically into a discussion of Russian and French films. He turned to his own
drink and threw it down quickly; the Scotch had burned
his throat, settled in his stomach, diffusing warmly its po-
tent mystery.

She was coming! He was going to see her again after
all these years . . . Edna. His little wife . . .

Wesley lit up a cigarette and inhaled the smoke deeply,
bitterly: he could feel the mellow wound in his lungs, the
tang in his nostrils as the smoke slipped out in thin double
spurts. He blanked the cigarette viciously.

What the hell did she want? Hadn't she fouled up
everything enough? A little fool, she was, a crazy one if
there ever was . . . and he had married her ten years ago at
seventeen, the worse simpleton in town, marrying one of
those silly summer tourist's daughters, eloping in a blind
drunk.

Well, they had settled down fairly well just the same . . .
that flat on James Street with the cute little kitchenette.
And his old man had raised his garage salary to thirty
bucks, a good job with a cute wife waiting at home. Her
wealthy parents had given her up for crazy even though

they sent her a check every month enclosed with notes that suggested they hoped she wasn't living in squalor and filth!

Squalor and filth! Even though he was seventeen, just out of high school, he had had sense enough to take good care of his young wife. It was none of his doing that everything went wrong; Edna, at sixteen, was a wild little cuss. That night at the garage when the hospital called and informed him his wife had been seriously injured in an automobile accident near the New York-Vermont state line . . . was it his fault she went on drunken parties with a bunch of high school kids while he worked his hide off in Charley's garage? Mangled in a smashup with the baby five months along. And the crowning glory of all! . . . her family had her taken to a swanky hospital in New York and that old sonofabitch of an uncle of hers breezing up to the house and starting to raise a row. Charley just pushed him out the door and told him to go run up a tree.

Wesley glanced fondly toward his father who stood shaking a mixer and talking with the customers. Charley Martin, the greatest dad a guy ever had! He pushed Edna's old sonofabitch of an uncle out the door and told him to go run up a tree while Ma bawled and he had sat in the big chair, crushed and stunned by the accident, by the false accusals, by everything. Charley was the guy who pulled him through that one . . .

Ten years. He had worked a few extra weeks in the garage, crawling around in a trance, until Edna's first letters began to come from the New York hospital. She would recover and they would start all over again, she still loved him so much, she missed him, why didn't he come down to see her? Sure!—her rich folks would have loved that. Sure!—she loved him, she loved him so much she went wolfing around with high school kids while he worked in the garage nights.

Bah! He had done the right thing by just blowing. In the middle of the night, he had gotten up and walked through the streets, where the dark swishing summer trees seemed to be singing him a farewell song, and he had hopped the freight for Albany. That had been the start of it—ten years of wandering; Canada, Mexico, forty-three states, jobs in garages, lunchcarts, construction gangs, Florida hotels, truck driving in George, barkeep in New Orleans, spare hand around racing stables, going West with the big circus, touting at Santa Anita, bookie in Salem, Oregon, and finally shipping out on his first cruise from San Francisco. Then it had been those lazy days in the Pacific, around the Horn, all over the whole shooting match, from Japan to Dutch Guiana. Ten years . . . Meeting up with guys like

Nick Meade and rioting for the poor Indian stiffs in Calcutta; getting jailed in Shanghai for following Nick around—he was the Communist, all right . . . but he himself had done it for a good time and general principles where Nick believe in it; well, Wesley Martin would just as soon believe in nothing if it meant all the Goddamned fuss he'd been through; Nick was a good kid, he'd fought for the poor Spanish stiff and got lead for it; for his own taste, just going to sea was enough, was everything, to hell with riots and drinking and marriage and the whole shooting match. It was a matter of not giving a hoot in hell—the sea was enough, was everything. Just let him alone, he would go to sea and be in a world to his liking, a just, reasonable, and sensible world where a guy could mind his own business and do his equal share of the work.

And so what the hell was she after now? He'd seen her once before, in a New York night club, but she missed him when he beat it. To hell with her! He was through with the beach and anything connected with it . . .

Wesley refilled his glass, drank down, refilled it again, and drank down a second time. He would be so soused when she arrived he wouldn't recognize her . . . what did she look like now? Shuckall! . . . he was pretty drunk already. Maybe she looked like an old hag now, a half-smooched debutante with cocktail rings around her eyes.

In that New York night club, she'd looked a bit older, of course, but she still had the same figure, the same eager laugh . . . she was with a tall blond guy who kept fixing his black tie all the time: that was five years ago.

Wesley turned around and glanced toward the screen-door entrance . . . was she really coming? Had she really been waiting two months for him in Boston?

Wesley poured himself another drink; the quart was almost empty, so he refilled his two comrades' glasses—they were now discussing music—and emptied the bottle altogether of its contents; once more, he felt like smashing the empty bottle, as he had always done to this symbol of futility—after each surrender to its unfulfilled promises. He would like to smash it against all of the bottles in his father's bar and then pay him for the damage—perhaps he should have done just that in New York when he had eight hundred dollars, he should have gone down to the gayest bar in the city and smashed all the bottles, mirrors, and chandeliers, all the tables and trays and . . .

"Wesley?"

Wesley's heart leaped; his father, down at the end of the bar, was staring at the person behind him who had spoken. It was Edna . . . it was her voice.

Wesley turned slowly. A girl was standing behind him, a pale girl in a dark brown summer suit; a scar ran from her forehead down to her left eyebrow. She was a woman, a full-grown woman and not the little Eddy he had married . . . ten years ago . . . no, it was another woman.

Wesley could say nothing—he gazed into the searching blue eyes.

"It is Wesley!" she said, half to herself.

Wesley couldn't think of anything to say; he sat, head turned around, gazing dumfoundedly at her.

"Aren't you going to say hello?"

"You're Edna," he mumbled hypnotically.

"Yes!"

Wesley disengaged himself slowly from the bar stool and stood facing the girl, still holding the empty quart bottle. His hands were trembling. He could not tear his astonished gaze from her face.

"How have you been, Wesley?" she asked, straining to be formal as best she could.

Wesley said nothing for a few seconds, his eyes wide with stupefaction; he swayed slightly on his feet.

"Me?" he whispered.

The girl moved her feet nervously.

"Yes, how have you been?" she repeated.

Wesley glanced quickly toward Bill Everhart and Nick Meade, but they were so engrossed in their discourses, and so drunk, they hadn't even noticed the presence of the girl. His father was watching from the other end of the bar, frowning his bushy white eyebrows together in what seemed to Wesley an expression of embarrassed anxiety.

Wesley turned to the girl.

"I'm fine," he managed to stammer.

They were silent, facing each other uncertainly in the middle of the sawdust floor.

"Please," said Edna at length, "will you . . . would you care to . . . take me outside?"

Wesley nodded slowly. As they walked out, he stubbed his toe and almost fell—he was drunker than he had figured—drunk as hell.

They were out on the sea-smelling night street; an elevated roared a few blocks down, fading in the distance. The music and a rush of warm beer wind emptied into the night from the tavern.

"Let's walk," suggested Edna. "you're not feeling too well."

Wesley found himself strolling down a side street with Edna, her brown hair glistening beneath the lamps, her heels clicking primly in the soft silence.

"I'll be damned!" he muttered.

"Yes?"

"I'll be damned."

Suddenly Edna laughed, the same eager little laugh he had almost forgotten.

"Is that all you have to say?" she asked brightly.

Wesley realized he was still holding the empty quart, but he only studied it foolishly.

"What will people think?" laughed Edna. "A man and a woman walking down the street with a whisky bottle!"

He placed the bottle in his other hand and said nothing.

"Here, let me put it down," said Edna. She put her hand over his and gently took the bottle . . . her touch startled him. She placed it carefully in the gutter as he gazed down at her stooped figure. When she straightened up, she was standing very close [to] him.

Wesley felt suddenly very drunk—the pavement began to slide from beneath him.

"You're going to fall!" she cried, clutching his arm. "My God, how much did you drink?"

He put his hand to his brow and realized he was streaming with cold perspiration. His jaw was trembling.

"You're sick," cried Edna anxiously.

"I drunk quick," grunted Wesley.

Edna dragged his shuffling figure to a doorstep: "Sit down here." He dropped heavily and put his hands to his face; she sat down beside him quietly and began to stroke his hair with strange, tender fingers.

They said nothing for a good many minutes while Wesley kept his hands to his face. He heard an auto roll by.

Then she spoke.

"You've been going to sea?"

"Yeah."

"I wrote to your brother years ago and he told me. He's married now."

"Yeah."

"He told me your father had opened a business in Boston and that you went to see him once in a while."

Silence.

"Wesley, I've been looking for you ever since. . ."

He shot a quick glance in the other direction and then resumed a fixed study of the warehouse across the dark street.

"You never left a trace, not even in the Union hall. I wrote you many letters . . . did you receive them?"

"No."

"You didn't?"

"I never bothered to ask," he muttered.

"Why you must have dozens of letters waiting for you in the New York hall."

He was silent.

"Are you feeling better?" she asked.

"Yeah."

"A little fresh air. . . ."

A cat prowled by, a lean rangy cat. Wesley remembered the little kitten he had found on Broadway a few nights before, this cat was older, more abused, hardened, starved: he was not helpless . . . like the kitten.

"Do you want to know why I've been looking for you?" Edna suddenly asked.

Wesley turned his dark eyes on her: "Why?"

Before he knew what had happened, her lips were pressed against his mouth, her arm had clasped around his neck. Dimly, he recognized the taste of her mouth, a fragrant tang that swooned his senses with a recollection of things he had not known for eras in his life, and which now returned to him in a tremulous wave of loss. It was Eddy again! . . . it was 1932 again! . . . it was Bennington again, and the swishing trees outside their bedroom window again, and the mild Spring breeze sighing into the garage again, and a youth in love again!

"I still love you, Wes, and you know damned well I always will!" she was whispering huskily, angrily in his ear.

Her husky whisper again! The sun, the songs again!

"I do! I do, Wes!" her savage whisper was saying.

Wesley clutched her yielding shoulder and kissed her. What was this ghost returning from the hollow corridors of time? Was this little Eddy, beautiful little Eddy he had taken for his wife in another time, the ill-starred little tourists' daughter he had met at a summer dance and loved on the shores of his boyhood pond, on the sands beneath a long ago moon—a strange, secret, happy moon?

Her lips were fragrant, moving; he tore his mouth away and sank it in the cool waves of her hair. The same sweet hair! The same sweet hair!

Edna was weeping . . . the tears were rolling down the back of Wesley's hand. He turned up her face and gazed at it in the somber darkness, a pale visage gemmed with tears, a strange face that tore his heart with a tragic, irrefragable sense of change. This was not she! Once more she had drawn his face to hers; a wet mouth was kissing his chin. His cheek, pressed against her feverish brow, could feel a dull throbbing in the furrow of her scar. Who was this woman?

A deep ache sank into Wesley's breast, an intolerable ache that crept to his throat. It was Eddy of course! She had weaved back into that part of him that was still young, and now she stunned that part of him that was old, she stole into it, a stranger haunting his life. He jumped to his feet with an angry cry; half snarl, half sob.

"What the hell do you want?" he quavered.

"You!" she sobbed.

He put his hand to his eyes.

"Don't give me that!" he cried.

She was sobbing on the steps, alone. Wesley took out his cigarettes and tried to extract one from the deck. He couldn't. He flung the pack away.

"I want you!" she wailed.

"Go back to your rich boyfriends!" he snarled. "They got everything. I ain't got nothing. I'm a seaman."

Edna looked up angrily: "You fool!"

Wesley didn't move.

"I don't want them, I want you!" cried Edna. "I've had dozens of proposals . . . I waited for you!"

Wesley was silent.

"I'm glad you're a seaman! I'm proud!" Edna cried. "I don't want anybody but you—you're my husband!"

Wesley wheeled around; "I'm not stoppin' you—get a divorce!"

"I don't want a divorce, I love you!" she cried desperately.

Wesley looked down and saw the empty quart bottle at his feet. He picked it up and hurled it away; it shattered explosively against the warehouse wall across the street, popping like a light bulb. Edna screamed sobbingly.

"That's what I think about the whole thing!" shouted Wesley.

A window opened above, a woman in a sleeping gown thrusting her head out adamantly: "What's going on down there?" she shrilled suspiciously.

Wesley wheeled about and faced up.

"Close that Goddamned window before I pop it!" he howled at the lady.

She shrieked and disappeared.

"I'm goin' to call the police!" threatened another voice from a newly opened window.

"Call 'em, you old tub!" shouted Wesley. "Call out the Marines . . ."

"Oh Wes you'll be arrested!" Edna was pleading in his ear. "Let's get away from here!"

"I don't give a hootin' hollerin' hell!" he cried, addressing the whole street in general.

"Wesley!" pleaded Edna. "Please! You'll be arrested . . . They'll call the police!"

He spun toward her: "What do you care?"

Edna clutched his shoulders firmly and spoke directly in his face: "I do care."

Wesley tried to free himself from her grasp.

"It's too late!" he snarled. "Let me go!"

"It's not too late," she persisted. "We can make it just the same again . . ."

Wesley shook his head savagely as though he were trying to rid himself of confusions.

"Can't! Can't!" he quavered. "I know!"

"Can!" hissed Edna.

"No!" he shouted again. "I'm not that same anymore . . . I changed!"

"I don't care!"

Wesley was still shaking his head.

"Please, Wes, let's go away from here," Edna cried, her voice breaking in a voluptuous sob.

"Can't!" he repeated.

"Oh you're too drunk to know what you're doing," wailed Edna. "Please, please come away . . ."

All along the street, windows were open and people were jeering down at them. When the police car rounded the corner, a man called: "Jail the bums!" and all his neighbors took up the cry as the car pulled up below.

CHAPTER SIX

When Everhart awoke the next day, the first thing he was conscious of was a weird song being chanted from somewhere above. Then he opened his eyes and saw the white steel plates. Of course! . . . The *S.S. Westminster*: he had signed on a ship. But what of the song?

Everhart vaulted down from the bunk, clad simply in his shorts, and poked his head out of the porthole. It was a hot, hazy day, the sun bearing down in shimmering rays on the mellifluous waters of a steaming harbor.

Bill peered up but could see nothing save the sweeping bulge of the ship's hull and the underside of a lifeboat. The strange singer was still chanting, perhaps from the next deck, chanting, it seemed to Bill, a song of the Far East— yet definitely not Chinese.

Bill pulled his head in and groaned: he had a big head from drinking too much and arguing too much with

Meade the night before. He turned to Eathington, who lay reading the Sunday funnies in his bunk.

"Haven't you a hangover from last night?" asked Bill with a trace of hopeful anticipation.

"Nah."

"Who the hell is singing upstairs? It makes my flesh creep . . ."

"Up above," corrected Eathington.

"Well who is it?"

Eathington folded his paper back: "The third cook."

"Tell me, haven't you a headache? You were with us last night!" persisted Bill.

"Nah."

"Who is the third cook? Is he Korean? Burmese?"

"He's a Moro," corrected Eathington. "When he gets mad he throws knives. A Moro tribesman."

"Throws knives? I don't believe it!"

"Just wait," observed the young seaman. "He's a Moro from the Philippines. They go around with knives between their teeth." And with this, he went back to his Sunday comics.

Bill dressed leisurely. He went back to the porthole and watched the seagulls swoop above the wharves. The water beneath the dock piles lapped quietly against the cool, mossy timbers. From somewhere in the ship, deep in its vaulted structure, he heard the muffled idling boom of a great engine.

He went down the cool gangway, acrid with the smell of fresh paint, and climbed up to the poop deck. Several seamen were calmly reading the Sunday papers in the shade. The deck was littered with newspapers, great coiled cables of hemp, pillows, abandoned folding chairs, cans of paint, and two or three empty liquor bottles. He knew none of the seamen.

He walked forward along the deck, marveling at the sweep of its superstructure curving toward the bow in a massive coordination of timber. At the bow, he peered down the side at the oily waters far below. Directly beneath him hung a gigantic anchor, drawn to the side of the ship by a super chain leading through an opening in the port bow. The seamen, thought Bill with a smile, were prone to call this huge mass of steel "The hook."

He strolled aft and gazed up at the bridge: slits in the gray wall peered out from the bridge house, where the captain would direct the voyage to Greenland—that would be where Wesley, as an able bodied seaman, would take his turn at the wheel and compass. God! If Everhart could do that rather than serve hungry A.B.'s and wash their dishes! He would have to begin his duties Monday—the next day— he hoped the work would prove pleasant enough.

"Thinking of Wesley, by the way," thought Everhart, "where the devil did he wander off to last night? He must be in his focastle or eating in the galley . . ."

Bill went below to the galley. It was crowded with all sorts of people he did not know, seamen eating and chatting noisily. Where was Wesley? Or Nick Meade? Not a familiar face in the lot . . .

Bill went forward down the narrow gangway. He found Nick Meade in the small P.O. mess drinking a cup of coffee with a haggard scowl.

"Meade!" greeted Everhart with relief.

"Yeah," mumbled Nick, passing this vague remark off as a greeting. He rose and refilled his cup from an aluminum coffee urn.

"How are you feeling?" grinned Bill.

Nick shot him a contemptuous scowl: "Do I look happy?"

"I'm feeling lousy myself . . . God, it's tough to have a hangover on a hot day like this!" Bill laughed, seating himself beside Nick. "Some night, hey?"

Nick said nothing; he drank his coffee sullenly.

"Did you see Wesley?" pressed Bill nervously.

Nick shook his head.

"I wonder where he is," worried Bill out loud. "Did you notice him wander off last night?"

Nick shook his head again. He finished his coffee and rose to leave.

"Where are you going now?" asked Bill, embarrassed.

"Bed," mumbled Nick, and he was gone.

Bill grinned and rose to pour himself some coffee in a clean cup from the rack. Well! He'd better prove himself a complete Communist before he could get a rise out of Mr. Nick Meade . . . he seemed to be quite averse to Mr. Everhart. What in heavens was the matter with the man? On their way back to the ship at dawn, after staying late drinking in Mr. Martin's room above the tavern, Nick hadn't said a word. They had passed the wharves, where the flames of a hot, red morning had played upon the masts of fishing smacks and danced in the blue wavelets beneath the barnacled docks, and neither had spoken a word. They had parted at the gangplank, where Bill had managed to bid Nick good morning, but the other had only glided off quickly, half asleep, and quite ill-tempered. Perhaps it was only his characteristic attitude after drinking, and perhaps too it was because he didn't consider Everhart sufficiently left wing. If that was the fool's attitude, he could jump in the drink! And yet, perhaps Bill was arriving at nervous conclusions . . .

It had been pleasant enough so far, but now he was beginning to dislike the whole idea. The ship swarmed with strange, unfriendly faces—and no Wesley. Where was he? By George, if Wesley had gone off somewhere, drunk, and wasn't to return to the ship . . . by George, he would not sail with the *Westminster*. He would manage to get back to New York somehow and go back to work . . . In heaven's name, this was folly!

Everhart left his coffee untasted and went forward.

"Where's Martin's focastle?" he asked a seaman in the narrow gangway.

"Martin? What is he?" asked the seaman.

"An A.B."

"A.B.? Their focastle is just forward."

"Thanks."

In the focastle, a tall curly haired man, sprawled in his bunk with a cigarette, did not know Wesley.

"When does this ship sail?" asked Bill.

The seaman gave him a queer look: "Not for a few days . . . mebbe Wednesday."

Everhart thanked him and walked off. He realized he was lonely and lost, like a small child . . .

He went back to his focastle and threw himself on the bunk, tormented with indecision. What manner of man was he? . . . couldn't he face reality—or was it that, as a professor, he was only capable of discussing it?

Reality . . . a word in books of literary criticism. What was the matter with him!

He awoke—he had slept briefly. No! It was dark outside the porthole, the light was on . . . he had slept hours, many hours. In his stomach he felt a deep emptiness, what ordinarily should have been hunger, but which seemed now nothing more than tension. Yes, and he had dreamed—it seems his father was the captain of the *Westminster*. Ridiculous! Dreams were so irrational, so gray with a nameless terror . . . and yet, too, so haunting and beautiful. He wished he were home, talking to his father, telling him of the dream.

A heavy wave of loneliness and loss swept through him. What was it? A loss, a deep loss . . . of course, Wesley had not returned to the ship, Wesley was gone, leaving Bill alone in the world he had lead him to. The fool! Didn't he have feelings, didn't he realize that . . . well, Everhart, what didn't he realize?

Bill mumbled: "What a silly child I'm being, no more sense nor strength of purpose than Sonny . . ."

"Are you talkin' to yourself again?" Eathington was asking, with a note of sarcasm.

Bill jumped down from the bunk, saying firmly: "Yes, I was. It's a habit of mine."

"Yeah?" grinned Eathington. "He talks to himself—he's a madman!" Someone laughed quietly.

Bill turned and saw a newcomer lying in the lower berth beneath Eathington. He was tall and thin, with blond hair.

"Don't annoy me, Eathington," Bill snapped testily from the sink.

"Don't annoy me!" mimicked Eathington with his puckish smile. "See . . . didn't I tell you he was a professor!"

Bill felt like throwing something at the kid, but at length convinced himself it was all in good fun. The newcomer chuckled nervously . . . he was apparently trying to keep in good graces with both of them. Eathington, Bill mused was the sort who would need an accomplice for his sarcastic nature.

"Has anyone a cigarette?" asked Bill, finding he had none left in his pack.

"Jesus! Bummin' already!" cried Eathington. "I can see now here I'm gonna move out of this focastle . . ."

The blond youth was rising from his bunk. "Here," he said in a polite, low voice. "I have some."

Bill was astounded at the sight of him. The youth was, in truth, a beautiful male . . . his blond hair was matted heavily in golden whorls, his pale brow was broad and deep, his mouth full and crimson, and his eyes, the most arresting part of his appearance, were of a shell-blue, lucid quality—large eyes and long eyelashes—that served to stun the senses of even the least perceptive watcher. He was tall, thin, yet possessed of a full-limbed physique, a broad chest, and square shoulders . . . his thinness was more manifest from the stomach down. Bill found himself staring rather foolishly.

"Have one?" offered the youth, smiling. His teeth were flashing white, a fact Bill had anticipated unconsciously.

"Thanks."

"My name's Danny Palmer—what's yours?"

"Bill Everhart."

They shook hands warmly. Eathington leaned on his elbow watching them with some stupefaction; obviously, he had cast lots with two professors rather than one; for the present, however, he decided to maintain a watching silence, and thus ascertain whether his convictions should crystallize.

The blond youth sat on one of the stools. He wore blue dungarees and a silk sport shirt; on his wrist he wore a handsome gold watch, and on his left hand an expensive looking ring.

"This is my first trip," Palmer confessed cheerfully.

"Mine also," said Bill, grinning. "What sort of job did you get?"

"Scullion."

"Do you think you'll like it?"

"Well, I don't care; for now I'll be satisfied with any-thing."

"Is that a class ring you're wearing?" inquired Bill.

"Yes—prep school. Andover . . . I was a fresh at Yale last term."

"I see; and you're joining the Merchant Marine for the duration?"

"Yes," smiled Palmer. "My people don't like it—would rather have me stay in the College Officers' reserves—but I prefer it this way. I wouldn't care to be an officer."

Bill raised a surprised eyebrow.

"What were you?" inquired Palmer politely.

"I was Columbia myself," answered Bill, grinning at his own sophomoric remark. "I teach there as well."

"You do?"

"Yes . . . English and American Lit, in the University."

"Oh God!" laughed Palmer smoothly. "My worst sub-ject. I hope you won't ask any questions about Shake-speare!"

They laughed briefly. Eathington had turned over to sleep, obviously convinced of his suspicions.

"Well," put forth Bill, "I hope we both enjoy the trip, excitement and all . . ."

"I'm sure I will. This is my idea of going to sea. I've yachted to Palm Beach with friends and had my own punt in Michigan—I'm from Grosse Pointe—but I've never really sailed far out."

"Neither have I . . . I hope I don't get too seasick!" laughed Bill.

"Oh, it's a matter of not thinking about it," smiled Palmer. "Just make up your mind, I suppose, and you won't be sick at all."

"Surely . . . that sounds reasonable."

"Where are you from?"

"New York," answered Bill.

"Really? I go there quite often . . . we have a place near Flushing. Strange, isn't it, we meet here and probably passed one another in New York streets!"

"That's true," laughed Bill.

They chatted on easily for awhile until Bill remembered he must see if Wesley had returned.

"Well, I've got to go dig up my friend," laughed Bill. "Are you staying here?"

"Yes, I think I'll get some sleep," answered Palmer rising with his friendly, flashing smile. "I had quite a time of it at Harvard Square last night with friends."

"Harvard, hey?" laughed Bill. "I'll wager less debauching goes on there than at Columbia . . ."

"I don't doubt it," purred Palmer.

"Oh, there's no doubt about it!" leered Bill. "I'll see you later, Palmer. I'm glad I met you . . ."

"Same . . . goodnight."

They shook hands again.

Bill went up to the poop deck grinning to himself. At least, he had one friend to whom he could talk to, a polite, cultured youth fresh from Yale, even though he might prove a fop. He certainly was a handsome boy.

Bill tripped over a form on the deck. It was a seaman who had decided to sleep in the open.

"Sorry," muttered Bill sheepishly. He was answered with a sleepy protesting groan.

Bill walked forward. Voices from the mess hall below. Bill went down and found groups of seamen conducting numerous dice games; one of these men, with a roll of bills in one hand and dice in the other, sprouted a full beard. Some others were drinking coffee.

Bill strolled into galley, where others stood about chatting, but he could find no familiar faces. From one of the cauldrons came an aroma of rich, meaty stew; Bill peered down into the pot and realized he hadn't eaten all day. No one seemed to be paying any attention to him, so he chose a clean bowl from the dish rack on the sink and ladled out a brimming portion of beef stew. He gulped it quickly in the mess hall, watching, as he ate, the progress of the dice games. Considerable sums of money were changing hands, but no one seemed to think much of it.

Bill put his empty bowl in the sink and moved on down the galleyway. The big cook, Glory, was coming toward him, smoking his corn cob pipe.

"Hello Glory!" ventured Bill casually.

"Hello there son!" moaned Glory melodiously. "You layin' down a hipe?"

"Not tonight," grinned Bill.

Glory's face broke into a broad, brilliant smile.

"Not tonight he sez!" Glory howled thunderously. "He's not layin' down a hipe!" The big cook placed a hand on Bill's shoulder as he passed.

"No hipe tonight!" Glory was booming as he went off. Bill heard his deep basso chuckle come back to him down the galleyway.

"A remarkable personality," mumbled Bill with delighted astonishment. "And what a remarkable name— Glory! The glory that is Glory, indeed."

In the P.O. mess, where he had found Nick Meade earlier in the day, three strangers sat playing a stoical game of poker. None of them had seen Wesley.

"Well, could you tell me where Nick Meade's focastle is?" pressed Bill.

"Meade?" echoed one of them, raising his eyes from the silent game of cards. "The oiler with the Crown Prince moustache?"

"That's him," grinned Bill nervously.

"He has a stateroom on the next deck, number sixteen." Bill thanked him and left.

He went forward toward Wesley's focastle; he might have just returned and gone to sleep unnoticed. But no one had seen him. One of the deck hands, a youth who might have been sixteen years old, told Bill he had shipped with Wesley before.

"Don't mind him," the boy grinned. "He's probably out on a long toot . . . he drinks like a tank."

"I know," laughed Bill.

"That's his berth," added the boy, indicating an empty bunk in the corner. "He's got a new toothbrush under his pillow. If he doesn't come back, I take it."

They laughed together quite cheerfully.

"Well, in that case, I hope he does come back," Bill said. "He bought that toothbrush just yesterday on Scollay Square."

"Good!" grinned the boy. "It oughta be a good one."

Bill ascended to the next deck. It was dark, quiet. From the harbor a barge shrilled a thin blast, shattering the Sunday night stillness with a brief, sharp warning. The sound echoed away. Bill could feel the *Westminster*'s engines idle way below, a passive heart gathering energy for a long ordeal, thrumming deeply a patient tempo of power, tremendous power in repose.

He found stateroom sixteen by the light of a match and rapped quietly.

"Come on in!" a muffled voice invited.

Nick Meade was stretched in his bunk reading; he was alone in the small stateroom.

"Oh, hello," he greeted with some surprise.

"Reading?"

"Yes; Emil Ludwig's *Staline* . . . in French."

Bill sat on a folding chair by the sink. It was a neat little room, considerably more homey than the steel-plated focastles down below, with soft-mattresses bunks, cabinet mirrors over the sink, and curtains on the blacked-out portholes.

"Pretty nice in here," said Bill.

Nick had resumed his reading. He nodded.

"You haven't seen Wesley yet?" Bill asked.

Nick looked up: "No. Don't know where in hell he is."

"I hope he didn't forget all about the *Westminster*," grinned Bill.

"Wouldn't put it past him," mumbled Nick, going back to his reading.

Bill took a cigarette from the pack on Nick's bunk and lit up in silence. It was stuffy in the room. He helped himself to a drink of water and sat down again.

"Know when we sail?" asked Bill.

"Few days," mumbled Nick, still reading.

"Greenland?"

Nick shrugged. Bill rose nervously and fidgeted about the room with his cigarette; then he wheeled and glared angrily at Nick, but the latter calmly went on with his reading. Bill walked out of the stateroom without a word and found himself back on the dark deck. He leaned on the rail and peered down gloomily; the water was slapping gently against the ship's waterline, an odor of decomposing, mossy timber rising from the darkness.

That blasted fool Meade! . . . And yet, who was the bigger fool of the two? Everhart, of course . . . he should go back in there and give him a piece of his mind. It would create a row, and God knows rows and arguments were unpleasant enough, but nothing could cure this humiliation but a man-to-man showdown! The fool was being deliberately annoying . . .

Bill, before he could reflect, found himself walking back into Nick's stateroom.

Nick looked up in bland surprise: "what'd you do, spit over the side?"

Bill found himself trembling neurotically, his knees completely insecure; he flopped back into the chair in silence.

Nick went back to his reading as though nothing was happening, as though Bill's presence was as casual and informal a fact as the nose on his face. Bill, in the meantime, sat shaking nervously in the chair; he raised a trembling hand to adjust his glasses.

"I met a boy from Yale on board," he told Nick in desperation.

"Quite a strikingly handsome chap."

"Is that so?" Nick mumbled.

"Yes."

There was a deep silence; the engines were pulsing below.

"Look here Meade!" Bill heard himself shouting. Nick looked up with a start, laying down the book.

"What?"

"You're holding my theories against me . . . I don't care personally . . . but it makes you look foolish!" Bill stammered.

Nick's blue eyes widened with stupefied resentment.

"You're too important a person to act like a child . . ."

"Okay!" interrupted Nick. "I heard you!"

"Well, do you admit it?" Bill cried from his chair. "Do you? If you don't you're a Royal fool!"

Nick's impassive eyes were fixed on Bill's, frozen to a cold blue.

"Ever since last night, you've been playing the angry and noble martyr." Bill rushed on in a nervous fever, hands trembling violently. "By George, I'll have you know I'm just as much anti-Fascist as you are, even though I haven't had the opportunity to shoot any in Spain!"

Nick's face had flushed, but his eyes retained their fixed frigid intensity, half angry, half fearful . . . indeed, Bill's quavering voice sounded slightly maniacal.

"Well?" Bill shouted chokingly.

"I wonder," Nick purred with contemptuous suspicion.

Bill jumped to his feet and stalked to the door.

"Oh!" he cried, "You're a privileged anti-Fascist, you are! You're the only one in the world!"

Nick stared rigidly at the other.

"You wonder!" mimicked Bill in a rage. "By George, you're not worthy of the movement . . . you're a confounded fool!" Bill tore open the door and plunged into the darkness, slamming the door with a smash.

He stumbled down the deck, choking with anger and humiliation; a mad satisfaction filled him despite all, the blood beating at his temples and intoxicating his whole tumultuous being in a hot rush of gratified rankle.

A voice was calling his name. Bill halted and turned around . . . it was Nick.

"Don't be a dope," he was yelling from his stateroom entrance. "Come back here."

Bill stood clenching his fists spasmodically.

"Come on, Everhart!" Nick was laughing. "You're a hot-headed reactionary, you are!"

"I am not a reactionary," Bill fairly screamed.

Nick was laughing convulsively. Bill turned and stumbled away, muttering under his breath.

"Where are you going?" Nick cried, still laughing. "You know I was only kidding!"

Bill was almost at the poop deck.

"See you tomorrow!" Nick was calling, hooting with laughter. Bill went down the hatchway and back to his focastle, stumbling over a stool as he entered.

Palmer was smoking a cigarette in his bunk.

"Don't kill yourself!" he laughed smoothly.

Bill growled something and vaulted up to his bunk; in five minutes he was asleep again, a deep, exhausted, sated sleep . . .

All night he dreamed chaotic tragic-comedies: Danny Palmer wore a dress and invited him to his bunk; Nick Meade was swinging from the ship's mast, hung by an enraged crew of pro-Fascists; and worse nightmare of all,

Wesley's funeral was being conducted on the poop deck, his body draped in a mottled bedspread was slid over the side and Everhart watched the body sink with horrified fascination; it seemed, also, that the *Westminster* was steaming past a tiny island upon which sat George Day in peaceful contentment, and that when Everhart waved and shouted at his friend, the ship lurched away from the island at a terrific speed. A voice woke Bill. He was in a cold sweat.

"Hey, feller, are you Everhart?"

Bill sat up quickly: "Yes!"

"Monday morning. You're deck mess boy. Dress up 'n come on down to the galley; I'll give you your duties."

Bill reached for his glasses: "Surely."

The man went away, but not before Bill caught a glance of him. He wore a Steward's blue uniform. Bill jumped down from his upper berth and washed up, glancing as he did through the porthole. It was very early morning; a cool mist raveled itself over the still, blue mirror of water. Bulls screamed and swooped in the morning sea air, nervously searching for their breakfasts, diving to the surface of the water and pecking quick heads to emerge in a fluttering ascent with dangling silver morsels. Bill, with his head out of the porthole, breathed deeply three times the thrilling, scented air. A red sun was just lifting over the harbor.

Bill dressed up in his old clothes and made for the galley in fine spirits. It was a beautiful morning . . . and a din of activity seemed to hum and clatter all over the *Westminster*. On the deck, seamen were sleepily engaged rolling up cables of rope, under the supervision of a gigantic First Mate with glasses. At the dock moorings, near the gangplank, shouting stevedores were rolling in more barrels of black oil, swinging in Army jeeps, carrying crates and boxes of all kinds. Bill looked around for familiar faces but found none. He went below.

The galley was in a turmoil over breakfast; all kinds of cooks and helpers Bill had never seen before on the ship were there, dressed in white aprons, wearing fantastic cook's caps; they slammed pots, shouted to one another, fried eggs and bacon at the range, roared with laughter in the confusion of steam, cooking smoke, clattering dishes, clanking pans, boom engines throbbing under; and dashed here and there in frantic haste found only in kitchens. Bill began to wonder where they'd all come from.

In the midst of all this noise, Glory's great voice moaned softly above all the rest as he walked calmly about his kitchen, with more dignity and acumen than the others, inspecting the sizzling bacon, opening pots and staring speculatively within, slamming shut oven doors. His booming basso was chanting, over and over again: "Every-body want to go to Heaven, but no one want to die!" He repeated this chant constantly, as though it were his litany for the new day.

Bill glanced around and saw the steward who had roused him; he was standing and watching the mad spectacle of the kitchen with saturnine approval. Behind him, a ray of young sunlight fell from the porthole. Bill went up to him: "Here I am," he grinned.

"Deck mess boy? You have nine A.B.'s to serve; get their orders from the galley here." The Steward motioned Bill to follow and lead him down the gangway to a small room starboard side. A table, covered with a checker cloth, stood in the center; in a corner was a battered old ice box.

"You serve them in here, three meals a day. Get the dishes from the galley. All your sugar, butter, vinegar, catsup and so forth is in this icebox. Keep it cold; the ice is in the refrigerator room near the galley. Get your aprons from the linen keeper forward to port."

The Steward lit up a cigarette quickly.

"I understand," said Bill. "I think I'll like this job."

The steward smiled to himself and left. Bill stood for a moment, undecided.

"Well, Professor Everhart, set the blasted table for breakfast!" he mumbled gleefully, and proceeded to do so

The Sea Is My Brother

with delighted alacrity. The Steward could afford to smile to himself, he knew very little about the little "deck mess boy," by George!

Bill had everything ready when the first A.B. came in for breakfast, yawning noisily and rubbing his ribs in a dejected morning attitude.

"What'll it be?" grinned Bill.

"Bacon n' eggs pal. Coffee n' juice."

When Bill returned with his breakfast, the seaman had fallen asleep on the bench.

After breakfast—everything had gone smoothly—Bill began to clear away the table, feeling quite at peace with the world and especially with his new job. It was paying him around two hundred dollars a month with room and board, and all he had to do was serve three meals a day! The A.B.'s had proved a fine lot and a quiet one at that. The only thing that worried Bill now was that Wesley hadn't been among them, and they were his focastle mates. He had obviously not returned—and perhaps wouldn't. Although he liked his job, Bill frowned at the idea of sailing alone—that is without Wesley—for he felt lost in the midst of so many strange, unfriendly faces. These seamen, he mused seemed to accept one another at face value, without fanfare and without comment. All this was so different from the keen sense of distinction and

163

taste which went with social life within academic circles. Perhaps the old adage, "We're all in the same boat" went without saying in the Merchant Marine and seamen resigned themselves to one another quite philosophically. And of course, like the slogan he had heard of—a famous placard above the door of the Boston Seamen's Club— which said, very simply, that all those who passed under the arch of the door entered into the Brotherhood of the Sea—these men considered the sea a great leveler, a united force, a master comrade brooding over their common loyalties.

As Bill was putting away the butter, Nick Meade put his head in the doorway.

"Good morning, old Tory!" he shouted.

Bill whirled around and stared; then he grinned: "Is that the way to talk to a worker?"

"A worker!" ejaculated Nick. "Now you can belong to the working class if not to the movement!"

Bill put away the butter to prove his station.

"You were a pretty hot Tory last night!" laughed Nick. He was wearing his engine room clothes—dungarees, white sandals, and an oil-smeared sweatshirt.

Bill shrugged: "Maybe I was . . . you had it coming."

Nick fingered his moustache.

"By Lenin! Were you ripping! I'll promise this time not to tell The Central Committee."

"Thanks."

Nick was gone as casually as he had come, padding away swiftly, down the alleyway, and whistling something very much like the Marseillaise.

Well, reflected Bill, Nick had proved himself reasonable after all, but it had taken plenty of his own nervous resources to bring it about. Perhaps he had been silly last night, but despite that he had succeeded in bringing Nick to his senses; the fact that Nick probably looked upon him now with some doubt as to his sanity meant less than what had been accomplished. A sorry fiasco! . . . but with results. It would teach Nick to stop being a Marxist Puritan. It should also teach Everhart himself to mind his own business and cease playing the wounded moralist, the fool . . . but he was not sorry he had blown up in such an undignified manner; it made him feel stronger; he had lived up to his convictions on human behavior. By George!—he was learning more than he ever had in any class.

When he had finished, Bill went back above to witness the loading on of the cargo. He walked jauntily down the deck. Danny Palmer was leaning on the rail with another seaman.

"Morning, Palmer," greeted Bill.

Danny turned his great blue eyes on Bill: "Hello, there." His hair flashed like warped gold in the sun. "How do you like your work?"

"Fine," chirped Bill.

They leaned and watched the operations below.

"Army Jeeps," mused Bill aloud. "I suppose we're bringing supplies to an Army base up there."

"That's right," said the other seaman, a short power-fully built Italian. "And we're taking back sick soldiers and Army base workers. See that lumber. That's for additional barracks. We're bringin' oil, lumber, food, dynamite for blasting, Jeeps . . ."

"Dynamite!" cried Danny.

"Shore! We get an extra bonus for that."

"The more money the better!" chatted Bill.

"Know something?" posed the seaman. "I heard we're sailing tomorrow morning instead of day after."

"Swell," purred Danny. "Who knows, we may be go-ing to Russia! Nobody really knows. These supplies may be for the Soviet Union."

"Russia, Iceland, India, South America, Persia, Texas, Greenland, Alaska, Australia," recounted the seaman monotonously, "—all the same; danger left and right. I got a buddie who went to Russia and come back to ship for Texas . . . and wham! Torpedoed off Virginia."

"That's the way it goes," said Bill moving off. "See you later, lads."

All along the deck, as Bill headed for Wesley's focastle, a pageant of activity unfolded. Stevedores were hastily putting the finishing touches on the *Westminster* before she sailed, painting on a new coat of camouflage gray, stringing and testing electric circuits, puttering here and there with plumbing, rehabilitating the complex component parts of the ship in a haste that suggested an early sailing to Everhart. Perhaps it was true about tomorrow morning—and what if Wesley shouldn't return by then?

As Bill was about to descend down the bow hatch leading to the deck crew focastle, he caught a glimpse of the captain of the *Westminster* as he stood before his bridge house chatting with the officers. He was a small round man, shorter by inches than any of his men, but the way they craned respectfully to his words belied his authority. From below, Bill could see the hard level eyes of the skipper, and very much like the ship's skippers in fiction, this little man with the heavily-striped sleeves had eyes like the color of the sea, pale misty blue with a suggestion of green, and the vague promise of tempest gray. A man among men! thought Bill. A man with a special wisdom of his own, and a knowledge of the sea that could confound all the books, chart all the lanes, and detect all storms, reefs, and rocks in a world of hostile oceans . . . it would be a fortunate privilege to talk to this man—perhaps he was the type of skipper who enjoyed chatting with his crew, and if this was so, Bill determined to watch for the opportunity to make his acquaintance. Was this the world he thought he had known about? Had it ever before occurred to him the high and noble meaning of so simple a station as the sea captain's?

Bill walked meditatively into the deck crew focastle. Wesley's bunk was still empty. He retraced his steps aft, pondering on his next move. In his focastle, he gazed emptily at his suitcase before he began to pack. Wesley had left for good—by George, then, he would not sail alone. The whole thing had been a farce in the beginning, the fruition of a nameless yen to sprout his wings and fly into life. Life was life no matter where one lived. He packed his clothes and snapped the catch shut. All he had to do was hand in his job slip at the union hall desk and get back to New York by hook or crook. He should have realized at first Wesley's deep-seated irresponsibility and lack of purpose; the man was no more than a happy-go-lucky creature to whom life meant nothing more than a stage for his debaucheries and casual, promiscuous relationships. He had lead Bill to this ship and then wandered off calmly as though all things in life were unworthy of too serious a consideration and application. What more should Bill have expected from Wesley? . . . he had proven himself quite convincingly in his cool rejection of Polly in New York that day they had started for Boston. God! Polly was perhaps still waiting for Wesley's call! Well, Bill Everhart wouldn't wait in vain for anyone . . . he'd never been that sort, and never would be.

Bill went up to the poop deck with his suitcase and stood for awhile watching the seamen arrange the cables in a great convoluted pattern on the deck. This was their medium, ships and the sea . . . it was no place for an academician. It was Wesley's medium, too, and not his own— his place was in the lecture room, where people conducted a serious study of life and strove to understand it rather than accept it with an idiot's afterthought, if any at all.

Behind him a ladder lead to the promenade deck. Bill put down his suitcase and clambered up; he found himself next to a great gun, its long barrel pointed toward the harbor. Several soldiers were busy oiling the gun at various points. Others were seated in folding chairs around the interior of the turret, reading papers and chatting. Bill peered silently at the gun; he had never been near so destructive a machine as this in all his life. It was a four-incher, and its graceful barrel was just then pointed ironically toward a destroyer in the middle of the harbor whose guns in turn were pointed toward the *Westminster*. Bill had not noticed the destroyer before—perhaps it had just slipped in, for her funnels were still smoking heavily. Perhaps, too, it was to be their convoy vessel, and it now sat patiently, waiting for sailing orders. Bill could discern small figures in white move in the confusion of the destroyer's gray hulk, a formidable warship manned by ingenious toy sailors, her mighty guns pointed in all directions, her flags flashing in the sun.

God! thought Bill . . . were the fleets of Xerxes ever as warlike as this super-destructive mammoth, a lean, rangy sea fighter proud with the fanfare of death?

Bill climbed another ladder and found himself topsides. Well, if he was leaving he might as well see it all! He gazed down at the *Westminster*'s big gun and followed the direction of its sleek barrel toward the distant destroyer. He tried to imagine the smoke and thunder of a great sea engagement, the smash of shells, the list of dying ships . . .

The warm sun beat down on the top deck as Bill strolled aft. He was gazing aloft at the *Westminster*'s stack when he bumped into a steel cable. It ran to a boom pulley and down to a lifeboat. Bill advanced curiously and inspected the interior of the lifeboat: there were canteens, boxes, kits, canvas sacks, weather-beaten life belts, and several long oars. In the event of a torpedoing, would he Everhart, have to spend days, even weeks drifting in one of these barks? It occurred to him he had not considered the extreme danger involved in all this; perhaps he had better leave after all . . . there was no virtue in rushing toward death, by George.

Bill went back to his suitcase on the poop deck and shuffled aimlessly forward. Nobody paid any attention to him, which was perhaps to his advantage; no one would miss him, and they would simply hire another deck crew mess boy and let it go at that. He, for his part, would return to his life's work in New York, and that would be that. There were other ways of searching for experience; for that matter, there were other ways to raise money for the old man's operation. He was in no immediate need . . .

Bill decided to go down to his focastle and pick up any object he might have forgotten in his haste to pack. Once down there he felt the need to lie down and think, so he vaulted up to his bunk and lit a cigarette.

Danny Palmer was combing his hair at the sink.

"Looks like we'll sail soon," he offered.

"Suppose so."

"You don't seem too eager!" laughed Danny, putting away his comb.

Bill shrugged and smiled: "Oh, it doesn't excite me too much."

"Yes, I suppose it is boring at sea sometimes. I'm going to do some reading, anyway, and I'll keep a diary. There's always a way to beat utter boredom."

"Boredom," said Bill, "is the least of my worries. I found out ennui was my mortal enemy years ago, and I've learned since then how to avoid it to some extent. I slip shrewdly around it . . ."

"Good for you!" grinned Danny. He wound his watch carefully.

Bill blew smoke rings with a troubled face.

"I still suspect we're headed for Russia," beamed Danny. "Murmansk or Archangel . . . and if so, I doubt if we'll have time to be bored. It's a notoriously hectic run. Have you met any seamen who've gone there?"

"Surely, two of them—Meade and Martin."

"Who's Meade?"

"He's the oiler with the Crown Prince moustache," grinned Bill slyly.

"I'd like to meet those two; I'd like some firsthand information on Russia."

"You would?"

"Oh yes! I'm as left-wing as my father is right!"

Bill leaned on his elbow.

"That's going some, I'll bet," he leered.

Danny raised a blond eyebrow: "Very," he purred. "The pater is in the steel business, the mater is a D.A.R., and all the relatives belong to the N.A.M."

"That should make you an anarchist," judged Bill.

"Communists," corrected Danny.

Bill leaned back on his pillow.

"I'm dying to go to Russia and speak to the comrades," resumed Danny, gazing through the porthole. "That's why I joined the Merchant Marine . . . I must see Russia"—wheeling to face Bill—"and by God I shall!"

"I wouldn't mind it myself."

"It's my ambition," pressed Danny, "my only ambition! I say, did you ever hear of Jack Reed?"

Bill faced Danny: "Jack Reed? The one who took part in the Revolution?"

"Yes! Of course! He went to Harvard, you know. He was great!" Danny lit up a cigarette nervously. "He died in Russia . . ."

Bill nodded.

"I'd like to . . . I'd like to be a Jack Reed myself some-day," confessed Danny, his blue eyes appealing sincerely to Bill's.

"A worthy ambition," said Bill.

"Worthy? Worthy? To believe in the Brotherhood of Man as he did?" cried Danny.

"Indeed . . . Reed was a great idealist, surely," Bill added, not wishing to seem unappreciative and dull. "I've always been inspired by his life, . . . He was truly a tragic figure and a great one at that. He gave up all his wealth for the cause. God! I wish I had as much conviction!"

"It's not hard to give up wealth," assured Danny. "It's harder to live for the movement and die in defeat, as he did."

"Agreed."

"Defeat," added Danny, "in the eyes of the world; but to Russia, and to all the comrades, it was no defeat . . . it was a supreme triumph!"

"I believe you're right—and I think it was, as you say, a supreme triumph in the estimation of Reed himself," supplied Bill.

Danny smiled enthusiastically: "Yes! You're right . . . tell me, are you a communist too?"

Bill grinned with some sarcasm.

"Well," he said, "I don't belong to the party."

"I meant . . . well, are you a communist in principle?" Danny pressed.

"I don't call myself a communist—I've never had occasion to, except when I was seventeen," admitted Bill. "But if you're asking me whether or not I lean to the left, my answer is yes—naturally. I'm not blind."

"Fine!" cried Danny. "Shake my hand, comrade!"

They laughed and shook hands, although Bill felt a great deal confused by it all. He had never been called "Comrade" before.

"We're probably the only ones on board," raced on Danny. "We must stick together."

"Oh yes."

"I suppose all the others either have no ideals or they're all reactionaries!" added Danny.

"Especially," leered Bill, "that oiler, Nick Meade. He hated Russia . . ."

"He did? Probably just a materialist."

"Yes . . . as a matter of fact, he's an iconoclastic neo-Machiavellian materialist," cooed Bill.

Danny glanced askance: "Am I supposed to know what that means?" Bill flushed.

"Of course not, I was only kidding Palmer. Tell you what, go down and find him in the engine room. He's really a communist."

"No!"

"Yes, he is," said Bill seriously. "He'll be glad to meet you . . . I'm certain of that."

"Engine room? Meade? Good, I'll go right down now," smiled Danny. "That makes three of us. God, am I relieved . . . I was hoping I'd find a few comrades, but I didn't bank much on it!"

Bill could say nothing.

"See you later, Everhart," called Danny, moving off. "Or is it comrade?" he added, laughing.

"By all means," assured Bill as cheerfully as he could. The youth was gone.

Bill flung his cigarette through the porthole.

"Comrade!" he spat. "What a priceless fool he turned out to be!" Bill flopped over viciously in his bunk and stared at the steel bulkhead. "Is the world full of fools? Can't anyone have sense just for a change?"

He glared fiercely at the bulkhead.

"I'm getting off this ship today, by George, before I go mad." He buried his face in the pillow and seethed with discontent; beneath, he began to feel a thin stream of remorse, like some cool agent attempting to allay the fire of his anger. He turned spasmodically to his other side; the coolness spread. He signed impatiently.

"Of course! I've been a fool again . . . Young Palmer was sincere and I wasn't . . . he's got ideals even though he makes a fool of himself by them. I should be ashamed of myself for being the sardonic skeptic—when the devil will I shed me of that Dedalusian ash-plant. It gets one nowhere, by George! I was only being a Nick Meade when I fooled with Palmer's naiveté and sincerity. The kid means well . . .

"A lesson in intolerance from Meade, that's all it was. If he's an orthodox Marxist, damn it, I go him one worse— an orthodox Everhartist. If they're not like Everhart, why, they're fools! Pure fools! And Everhart is the constant in an equation of fools . . . and I thought last night I was be- ing sensible when I let Nick have it—what a joke! I'm just as bigoted as he is."

Bill threw the pillow aside and sat up.

"I'll make it up with Palmer . . . he didn't notice my sarcasm, so the burden of reproach is mine and mine alone. By my soul! . . . a man can't go through life sneer- ing at his fellowmen—where will it get us!—we've all got to learn to respect and love one another, and if we're not capable of that, then, by George, the word has to be tolerance! Tolerance! If people like Nick don't tolerate me, then I'll tolerate them."

Bill leaped down to the deck and looked out the porthole.

"Otherwise," he mused gloomily, "nothing will ever change, not really . . . and change we must."

A seagull, perched on the edge of the dock platform, burrowed an exasperated beak in its feathers. Just beyond Bill could see the stern of the destroyer in the bay.

He nodded his head: "A hell of a time for tolerance! Or is it . . . a hell of a war for tolerance? They'll have to put it down in black and white before I believe it . . ."

Bill pulled his head in and poured himself a cup of water. He glanced at his packed suitcase.

"I should stick this out . . . just for principles. Theories and principles come to life only by application . . . theoretically, I'm opposed to Fascism, so I must fight it—Nick is on board, he's not turning tail. What would he think if I skipped off?" Bill grinned and opened his suitcase.

"All right, Mr. Meade, this laugh is on you."

He unpacked and lay down for a nap. Once more, as he dozed off, he began to feel jaunty.

"Do you know Martin?" a voice was asking him.

Bill woke up quickly.

"What time is it?" he asked. "I slept . . ."

"Almost noon," answered the seaman. "Look, a blond kid tells me you know a guy by the name of Martin."

"Yes, I do."

"Wesley Martin?"

"Yes."

The seaman handed Bill a note: "I don't know where to find him . . . will you give him this note?"

Bill scanned the outer folds of the note, where a hand had scribbled: "For Wesley Martin, A.B. seaman."

"A babe at the gate told me to give it to him," said the seaman. "I'd like to give it to her myself . . . she was some potato."

"A girl?"

"Yeah—at the gate. Give it to Martin; I'll see ya!" The seaman was leaving.

"I don't know where he is!" cried Bill.

"Well I don't neither—see ya later." The seaman strolled off down the alleyway.

Bill sat on a stool and tapped the letter speculatively; there was no harm in reading it, Wesley would never get it anyway. He opened and read:

Dear Wes,

I know now you'll change your mind. I'll be waiting for you. I love you.

Your wife

"Wife!" cried Bill aloud. "I thought he had left her . . ."
He re-read the note with a frown.

The steward was coming down the alleyway. Bill
looked up.

"Set your dinner plates," said the Steward. "It's almost
twelve."

"Right!" snapped Bill, rising. "I was sleeping."

He followed the steward back to the galley and
picked up his plates, cups, saucers, and silverware. On
the way to his deck crew mess he passed Danny Palmer,
who stood peeling potatoes with Eathington and another scullion.

"Did you meet Meade?" shouted Bill over the noise of
the noontime galley.

Danny smiled broadly and nodded with enthusiasm,
adding to that a significant wink of the eye. Bill grinned.
He carried the dishes to his little mess, where he com-
plimented himself for having signed up on a job where
he could work alone and in quiet. The galley was a always a clattering confusion; in his own mess, he could
set his table in peace and take the seamen's orders
calmly and carry them out with a minimum of dignity.
Surely . . .

"Hey there, man, don't split a gut!"

Bill swerved around and almost dropped the catsup. It was Wesley. And Wesley was gone as quickly as he had come. Bill hurdled a bench with a cry of surprise.

At the door, he called: "Hey Wes, come here!"

Wesley turned and shuffled back down the alleyway, smoking a cigarette: "I got to get back to work . . ." he began.

"This is a note for you," said Bill. "Where the devil have you been?"

Wesley flicked a corner of his mouth and took the note.

"I been in the can," he explained. "I raised hell an' got pulled in."

"Who bailed you out?" urged Bill.

Wesley was reading the note. When he'd finished reading it, he slipped it into his dungaree pockets and gazed at Bill with dark, stony eyes.

"Who bailed you out?" repeated Bill.

"Friend o' mine."

They stood watching each other in silence. Wesley stared at Bill intensely, as though he were about to speak but he said nothing.

Bill grinned and motioned toward his mess: "Service with a smile in here—ask the others."

Wesley nodded slowly. Then he placed a thin hand on Bill's shoulder.

"We sail in the morning, man," he said quickly, and went off down the alleyway without another word. Bill watched him disappear and then returned to his icebox. He could think of nothing to mumble to himself.

CHAPTER SEVEN

The Bosun was in at the crack of dawn to wake up the deckhands, but Curley was wide awake—he was still drinking from his bottle—and although he had sang all night up there in his top berth, none of the others had paid any attention to him. Now, while they were rousing themselves, Curley wanted know if anyone wanted a drink.

"Sober up, Curley, or the mate'll log you two, three days pay," Joe was saying as he pulled on his shoes.

"Lissen to me, guys," cried Curley, sitting up in his bunk and flourishing the bottle, "I'm never too drunk to do my work . . ."

Wesley inspected his teeth in the cracked mirror.

"You want a shot at this bottle, Martin?" cried Curley.

Joe scoffed: "You're all's too drunk to do anythin'."

Curley jumped down from his bunk with a curse, staggered over against a chair, and fell flat on the deck.

Wesley was right at his side: "Get up, Curley: I'll take a nip out of your bottle if you cut the bull."

"Cut the bull? I'll murder that Goddamned Joe for makin' that crack," howled Curley, pushing Wesley aside and trying to regain his feet.

Joe laughed and went to the sink.

Wesley pulled Curley to his feet and pushed him back to his own bunk. Curley swung his fist at Wesley but the latter blocked the punch with his forearm; then he threw Curley back on the bunk and pinned him down.

"Sober up, man," he said. "We got work to do; we're sailin' . . . I'll get you a wet towel."

"Get him another bottle!" suggested Haines from his bunk.

"I'll kill you, Joe!" shouted Curley, struggling in Wesley's grip. "Lemme go, Martin!"

"I thought you could hold your liquor better'n that, Curley," said Wesley, shaking his head. "An old cowpuncher like you. I'll bet you're too drunk to do your work . . ."

Curley pointed his finger in Wesley's face: "Lissen Martin, down in Texas a man's never to drunk to do his work. You lemme go—I got work to do."

Wesley let Curley up, but retained his hold on his arm.

Haines was peering out the porthole: "Christ! It's still dark out." The others were getting up.

Joe turned from the sink and drew on his shirt.

"Curley's been drunk for ten days," he announced. "Wait till the mate sees him up there; he won't be able to lift a rope or . . ."

"Shut up!" snapped Wesley. Curley was struggling to get at Joe, but Wesley had him pinned against the bulkhead.

"I'll kill you Joe! I'll split your lousy puss!" Curley screamed. "Lemme go, Martin, I'll kill him . . ."

"Who you tellin' to shut up, Martin?" demanded Joe quietly, advancing toward them.

"You," said Wesley, struggling with Curley. "This kid's drunk—we gotta fix 'em up."

"What the hell do I care about him?" purred Joe. "And who are you telling to shut up."

Wesley stared at Joe blankly.

"Huh?" pressed Joe menacingly.

Wesley flicked a smile and let go of Curley. In an instant, Curley was on Joe, slashing at him blindingly as Joe staggered back over a chair. Then they were on the deck, with Curley on top dealing out punch after punch into Joe's upturned face. The deck hands howled as they jumped out of bed to break it up. Wesley helped himself to a drink from Curley's bottle as the fists beat a brutal, bone-on-bone drumming on Joe's face. They tore Curley away, raging like a mad dog, and pinned him down in a bunk; Joe sat up and groaned pitifully, like a child in pain. He was bleeding at the mouth.

Wesley went to the sink and brought back a wet towel for Joe's face. Joe spat out a tooth as Wesley applied a towel carefully.

"Sober up that Curley," he told the others. "We'll all get hell now . . . sober up that crazy cowpuncher . . ."

Haines ran to the door and looked down the alleyway. "Bosun's not around . . . Christ! Hurry up before the mate comes below . . . throw water on him."

"Nice way to start a trip!" moaned Joe from the deck. "All cut up to hell. I know this ain't gonna be no trip. We're all goin' down."

"Ah shut up," scolded Haines. "You're punchy now."

Someone threw a glass of water on Curley's face and slapped him rapidly: "Sober up, Tex! We got to go to work . . ."

Wesley helped Joe to his feet: "All right, Joe?"

Joe stared blankly at Wesley, swaying slightly.

"I'm all cut up," he moaned.

"You shouldn't have been so right foolish!" said Wesley.

"I know, I know," groaned Joe. "I'm all cut up . . . I don't feel natural . . . somethins' gonna happen . . ."

"Will you shut up!" shouted Haines. Curley was sitting up blinking; he smiled at all of them and started to sing "Bury Me Not on the Lone Prairie"—but he was sober enough. They dragged Joe and Curley above and let them breathe in the cold dawn fog.

"Let's get to work," said Haines impatiently.

Joe staggered but caught himself in time.

"What a hell of a way to start the day," muttered Charley, the ordinary seaman. "Drunken bastarts . . ."

"All right, forget it!" snapped Haines.

The bosun was calling them aft. A gray dawn was fanning out across the sky.

"I'm sorry Joe," mumbled Curley. Joe said nothing. The *Westminster*'s stack was pouring out great clouds of black smoke as they reached aft, where the first mate, the bosun, and a Maritime deck cadet were waiting.

Down on the dock, longshoremen were unwinding the *Westminster*'s hawsers . . .

When Everhart woke up, he heard the booming blast of the *Westminster*'s stack. He jumped down from his bunk and stood in front of the open porthole—the wall of the dock shed was slipping by. Bill put his head out and gazed forward: the ship was backing out slowly from the slip, leaving a sluggish wake of whirlpools. Longshoremen and guards stood on the receding dock platform, watching, their work done.

Once more the *Westminster* roared her blast of departure, a long, shattering, deep peal that echoed and re-echoed in the morning quiet over the wharf-roofs, railroad yards, and buildings all along the waterfront.

Bill washed hastily and ran above. He felt great piston charges rumble along the deck, heard the giant churning of the propeller. As he gazed aloft at the *Westminster's* stack, she thundered for the third time—"Vooooom!"—and lapsed into quiet as the sound soared out over Boston's rooftops.

In the middle of the harbor, she stopped; then the propeller chugged again, the winch-engine rumbled below as the rudder was set, and the *Westminster* slowly and ponderously pointed her bow around to face the Atlantic. The winch screeched deeply once more—and they moved slowly, smoothly toward the mine net at the mouth of the harbor, the propeller chugging up a steady Gargantuan rhythm.

Bill hastened up to the bow and peered down at the prow, its sharp, steep point dividing the harbor water with the ease of power. The *Westminster* slipped on, faster and faster. Seaweed wriggled past lazily.

Bill squinted toward the sea. Far out, he saw, in the gray mist, a low, rangy shape . . . the destroyer, of course! They were on their way! And what a fool he would have been to miss this . . . !

They were nearing the mine net swiftly; and [an] opening had been made for them. As the *Westminster* slipped through, the sailors on the mine boats waved casually. Bill could not take his eyes off the floating mines, huge black, spiked globes strung from beach to beach along a line of unbelievably destructive doom . . .

The two lighthouses glided by with dignity, the last outposts of society. Bill stared aft at Boston's receding skyline, a sleepy Boston unaware of the great adventure being undertaken, a Boston spurting occasional clouds of industrial smoke, the gray buildings dour-faced in the July dawn.

Bill returned his eyes seaward. Far off, where the horizon, mist, and bilious green sea merged, Bill saw dark vestiges of night fading to a pale gray.

Directly forward, the destroyer steamed swiftly through the calm waters; already, it seemed to Bill, the destroyer was on watch, her guns flaring to all directions. Bill turned and glanced up at the forward gun turrets: two soldiers with earphones stood by the guns, eyes out along the horizon.

It was done! He could never go back now . . . Let come what may, they were prepared, and so was he . . .

"I'm never too drunk to do my work!" someone was yelling on the bow. Bill turned and saw Wesley, with two other deckhands, rolling up cables on the deck.

"You're damned right, man," Wesley said.

"I'll git drunk. I'll start fights, I'll do anything!" Curley cried in Wesley's face. "But I'll do my work. Am I right?"

"Shut up, will you?" Haines muttered.

"Well, am I right?" demanded Curley.

"Shore!" assured Wesley.

They went on rolling the cables in silence. When they were finished, Wesley lit up cigarette and gazed out over the waters.

"Morning Wes," greeted Bill.

Wesley turned and waved his hand solemnly.

"How do you like it?" he asked.

Bill leaned on the deck rail and squinted down at the water: "Exciting . . . this is my first time at sea, and I must say it gives me a queer feeling."

Wesley offered him a cigarette.

It was getting warmer; the mist had lifted, and now the long swells glistened luminously in the bright white light. Bill could feel the bow rise and fall in smooth, swishing strokes as the *Westminster* moved on.

"How is it," grinned Bill, "on the bow when the sea is rough?"

Wesley tossed his head with a smile: "You gotta hang on to something or you'll take a ride on the deck."

"Do you ever get seasick?" asked Bill.

"Shore . . . we all do one time or another," answered Wesley. "Even the skipper sometimes."

"Hey Martin!" cried Haines. "We gotta go below."

Wesley threw away his cigarette and shuffled off to his work. He wore the same moccasins he had when Bill met him in New York, plus a pair of paint smeared dungarees and a white shirt. Bill watched him go below with Haines and Curley; he was rubbing Curley's head playfully while Curley took up a new song with dramatic gestures.

"Seven years," howled Curley, "with the wrong woman . . . is a mighty long time . . ." then they disappeared down the hatchway.

Bill smiled to himself; he was glad to see Wesley happy again—that note from his wife the day before had obviously troubled him, for he hadn't come to mess all day. Wesley seemed at home and content now they were sailing, as though leaving port meant the cessation of all his worries, and heading out to sea a new era of peace and amenity. What a simple solution! Would to God Everhart could find freedom in so simple a process as that, could be relieved of vexation by so graceful an expedient, could draw comfort and love from the sea the way Wesley seemed to do.

Bill went aft and below to his work. When the table was set, Joe the A.B. shuffled in gloomily. His face was all bruised.

"What happened to you?" grinned Bill.

Joe looked up in angry silence and shot an irritated glance at the other. Bill placed a plate in his hand.

"What's for eats?" growled Joe.

"Oatmeal . . ." began Bill.

"Oatmeal!" spat Joe. "I can see where this is gonna be a lousy run, crummy food, no-good crew . . ."

"Coffee with it?" leered Bill.

"What the hell do you think?" cursed Joe. "Don't be so Goddamned foolish."

"How am I to know . . ."

"Shut up and get it," interrupted Joe.

Bill glared and flushed.

"Who you lookin' at?" purred Joe, rising.

"You don't have to . . ."

"Lissen Shorty," cried Joe in Bill's face. "Keep shut if you don't want to get hurt, understand?"

"You're a test case!" mumbled Bill.

Joe pushed Bill with the flat of his hand. Bill stared fearfully at the other, paralyzed in his steps; he almost dropped the plate.

"Don't drop the plates," Joe now grinned. "You'll have to pay for them yourself. C'mon, c'mon, don't stand there like a dope, Short Man, get me my breakfast."

Bill walked to the galley in a stupor. While the cook was filling Joe's plate, he decided to stand for his rights, and if it meant a row, then row it was! Bill walked quickly back to his mess, rousing his senses for the inevitable . . . but when he returned, a heated argument was in progress among the deckhands. Curley, Haines, Charley and Wesley were seated at the table.

"I'm sorry!" Curley was shouting, "but for krissakes don't keep bringin' it up. I ain't responsible for what I do when I'm drunk . . ."

"That's all right," Joe whined, "but you still cut me up bad, you and your Goddamned booze . . ."

"Why don't you forget it!" Haines groaned restlessly. "It's all over now, so forget it . . ."

"Peace! Peace!" Charley cried. "Haines is right . . . so from now on, shut up about it."

Joe waved his hand viciously at all of them.

Bill dropped the breakfast plate before him. So, it was Curley's work . . . good boy!

Joe looked up: "Look, Shorty, don't drop my plate like that again . . ."

Haines rose to his feet: "There he goes again. I'm getting the hell out of here!"

"Wait!" commanded Wesley.

Bill stood glaring down at Joe. When Joe began to rise to his feet, Wesley placed a hand on his shoulder and sat him down.

"Take your hands off me, Martin!" warned Joe, his eyes fixed askance on Wesley's hand.

Wesley sat down on the bench beside him and smiled.

"All right, Joe, I will. Now I want to tell you . . ."

"I don't wanta hear it!" snarled Joe. "If you don't like my company, get the hell out."

"Sure," minced Haines savagely, "I'm divin' over the side and swimmin' back to port."

"Look, man," began Wesley, "that's just the point . . . we're out at sea and that's that. We're not on the beach no more—there, we can fight, booze, nowhere all we want. But when we're sailin' . . ."

"I said I didn't want to hear it!" cried Joe.

"You're gonna!" snapped Haines. "Go ahead Martin . . ."

Wesley's face hardened: "When we're sailin', man, there's no more o' that beach stuff. We have to live together, and if we all pitch in together, it's right fine. But if one guy bulls it all up, then it's no shuck-all of a trip . . . all fouled up."

"Get off my ear," mumbled Joe morosely.

"I will when you get it! You smarten up and do your share and we'll all be happy . . ." Wesley began hotly.

"Who ain't doin' his share!" retorted Joe.

"Your share of cooperation," put in Haines.

"Yeah," said Wesley, "that's it . . . your share of cooperation . . . do that and we'll all be grateful."

Joe banged his fork: "Suppose I don't . . ."

Wesley rubbed his black hair impatiently.

"Didn't Curley cut me up? What'd I do?" Joe cried.

"You started it!" hissed Haines.

Joe was silent.

"Will you do that, man?" asked Wesley seriously.

Joe looked around with an expression of awe, gesturing toward Wesley: "Ain't he the one, though!"

"That's not the point," broke in Haines. "He's talkin' for all of us. We want a good trip and we don't want a jeep like you queering it all up."

Joe resumed his eating quietly.

"Guys like you go over the side, if they get crabby enough," added Haines calmly.

"No room for me here," groaned Joe.

"Shore is," said Wesley. "Just stop gettin' wise with everybody . . . get the sliver out of your pants."

Joe shook his head with slow resentment.

"That's all there is to it," said Haines. "We all pull together, see?"

"Sure, sure," snarled Joe.

"Let's shake and forget it," put forth Curley. Joe let him shake his hand without looking up.

"Bunch o' crabs," he muttered at length.

"We ain't crabs," objected Wesley. "You're the crab in this outfit. Now for krissakes cut it out an' act right with us all. We're at sea, man, remember that." Haines nodded his head in assent.

"How 'bout some grub!" cried Charley. Bill had been standing watching this tribunal of the sea in action with some wonderment; now he woke from his reverie with a grin and picked up his plates.

The seamen called their orders and tried to laugh it off, but Joe presently finished his breakfast and stalked out without a word. When he had gone, there was a strained silence.

"He'll pull out of it," said Wesley.

"He'd better," warned Haines. "He's got to learn sometime . . . he's at sea."

That first day out, the *Westminster* sailed on hundred miles offshore and then turned north in the wake of the convoying destroyer. It was a warm, windless day at sea, with a smoothly swelling sheen of ocean.

When Bill finished his work after supper, he went aft to his focastle and lay down for a smoke. Above him, in an overhead rack, he detected a piece of canvas. Bill pulled at it and withdrew a gas mask; he sat up and peered into the rack; there was a lifebelt there also, with a small red light attached.

"Keep them handy," counseled Eathington from his bunk. "I keep mine at the foot of my bunk. You got a knife?"

"No."

"Get one; you might need a knife in case you ever need to do some fast and fancy cuttin'."

Bill leaned back and drew from his cigarette.

"We get lifeboat drills from tomorrow on," continued Eathington, "and fire drills sometime this week. You know your boat and fire stations?" he added accusingly.

"No," admitted Bill. Eathington scoffed.

"They're up on a notice in the alleyway!" he sneered.

Bill went out and glanced at the notice; he found his name in a group assigned to lifeboat number six and fire station number three. Well, if it came to a torpedoing, there would be little time for reference to the notice, so he might just as well remember his lifeboat number.

Bill blanked his cigarette and mounted the hatchways; when he pushed it open he found himself on a moonlit deck. Black-out hatches would help very little tonight, he reflected—the destroyer could be seen in the moonlight ahead as clearly as in the daytime. Yet, it was dark enough to conceal a periscope, by George!

Someone nearby echoed his thoughts: "Look at that moon! Clear as day." Two seamen were leaning on the poop deck rail.

"They can see us, all right," laughed Bill.

The seaman grinned: "An' we can hear them!"

"Yeah," snarled the other seaman, "That's unless they cut their engine and just wait for us."

"They do that," admitted the other seaman. "No submarine detector can spot that."

"The moon," mused Bill. "Lovers want it but we certainly don't."

"That's a mouthful," said one of the seamen.

They were silent as Bill gazed at the wake of the ship—a ghostly gray road back to home, unwinding endlessly and lengthening with every turn of the propeller. He shivered despite himself.

"Well," said the seaman, "let 'em come."

Bill strolled forward. The air was cool and clean, charged with the briny thrill of the waters. The *Westminster*'s funnel, rocking gently in silhouette against the moon, discharged clouds of blue smoke and darkened the stars. Bill gazed longingly at The Big Dipper and remembered how he had studied this body of stars on quiet nights along Riverside Drive . . . they were far from New York now . . . and going farther.

He went below to Wesley's focastle. Curley held his guitar and strummed meditatively from his top berth while the others lounged and listened. Joe was at the mirror inspecting his bruises.

Curley began to sing in a nasal, cowboy voice.

"Martin here?" asked Bill.

Charley rose from his bunk and yawned: "He's standin' bow watch . . . I'm relievin' him in two minutes."

Charley picked up his jacket and strolled out. On the bow, Wesley stood with legs apart gazing out, his hands sunken in a peacoat, face turned up to the stars.

"Take over, Charley," he said. "Hello there man."

"Hello Wes," said Bill. "How about the game of whist with Nick?" Wesley took off his peacoat.

"Right."

They sauntered from the bow, where Charley took up his station with a noisy yawn and a loud, sleepy groan.

"Haines is at the wheel," said Wesley motioning toward the bridge house above.

"How's bow watch?" asked Bill, remember how lonely Wesley had looked standing at the head of the ship in the face of the night waters, an erect, brooding figure.

Wesley said nothing; he shrugged.

"Lonely standing there watching the water for two hours, isn't it?" pressed Bill.

"Love it," said Wesley firmly.

When they opened Nick's door, his light went out.

"Hurry the hell in!" cried Nick. "Don't stand there picking your nose in the dark."

When Bill closed the door after them, the stateroom was flooded with light. Nick and Danny Palmer were seated at a small card table.

"Ah!" cried Palmer. "Now we have a foursome."

Wesley threw his peacoat on the bed and lit up a cigarette, while Bill drew a chair to the table.

"What is it?" asked Nick, fondling his moustache.

"Suits me."

"Me too."

"Your watch finished?" Nick addressed Wesley.

"Yeah."

"How is it out?"

"Moon bright as hell."

"Bad night, hey?" smiled Palmer.

"Could be worse," grunted Wesley, pulling up a chair. "These ain't hot waters like the Gulf or off Newfie and Greenland."

Nick dealt the cards blandly.

"When's your engine room watch?" asked Bill.

"Midnight," said Nick. "We can play lots of games till then," he added mincingly. Palmer laughed.

They scanned their hands silently. Bill glanced at Wesley and wondered how he could watch the sea for hours and then coolly take part in a game of cards. Wasn't it a dark, tremendous thing out there on the bow? Wesley looked up at Bill. They stared at each other in silence . . . and in that brief glance from Wesley's dark eyes, Bill knew the man was reading his thoughts and answering them—yes, he loved and watched the sea; yes the sea was dark and tremendous; yes Wesley knew it and yes, Bill understood. They looked down.

"Pass," mumbled Danny, arching his blond brows.

"Check," said Wesley.

Nick rolled his tongue around his palate.

"Three," he said at length.

Bill waved his hand toward Nick. Nick grinned: "Are you giving me the palm?"

"Surely, the world is yours, Lenin," said Bill.

Danny laughed smoothly.

"How true," he purred.

"Diamonds is, trumps is," mumbled Nick.

They began to play in silence.

"I'm moving in with Nick," Danny presently announced. "Don't you think it's much nicer up here than down in that smelly focastle?"

"Surely," said Bill.

"Don't let him kid you," raced Nick. "Damn his excuses. He really wants to be near me."

Palmer laughed and blushed. Nick pinched his cheek: "Isn't he beautiful?"

Wesley smiled faintly while Bill adjusted his glasses with some embarrassment.

Nick resumed his play with a blank expression.

"No, but I really like it up here much better," Danny struggled. "It's much more pleasant." Wesley stared curiously at him.

Nick slapped an ace down with a smack. Smoke curled from Wesley's nose as he pondered his next move. The room was plunged into darkness as the door opened; they heard the waves outside swish and slap against the side of the moving ship.

"Don't stand there scratching your head!" howled Nick. "Close and come in." The door closed and the room was lighted again. It was one of the gun crew.

"Hello, Roberts," greeted Nick. "Sit ye down."

"I didn't know you ran a gambling hall," laughed the young soldier.

"Just whist."

The soldier perched himself up on Nick's bunk and watched the progress of the game. After a few minutes, Wesley rose.

"Get in the game, soldier," he said. "I'm pullin' out."

"You should," mumbled Nick.

Wesley ruffled Nick's hair. Bill put his own cards down: "Where you going Wes?"

"Stick around," cried Nick. "We need your foursome."

"I'm goin' down for a cup of coffee," said Wesley. He picked up his peacoat and went to the door.

"Hurry up!" said Nick. "I want to be in the dark with Danny." Danny laughed suavely.

Wesley waved his hand at Nick and opened the door; for a moment his thin frame stood silhouetted in the moonlit door: "Okay Nick?" he asked.

"Don't close it yet!" howled Nick.

When Wesley had left, they laughed and began a new game.

At ten o'clock, Bill left the game and made his way down to the galley. The mess hall was crowded with seamen playing dice and drinking coffee. Bill had a cup for himself; then he went back to the moon washed deck and watched the big yellow moon sink toward the horizon. He felt a wave of peace come over him . . . his first day at sea had proved as uneventful as it was casual. Was this the life Wesley had espoused? . . . this round of work, feeding, ease, and sleep, this mellow drama of simplicity? Perhaps it was the sort of thing Everhart had always needed. What he would do now is go to sleep, wake up, work, eat, hang around, talk, watch the sea, and then go back to sleep.

Nothing could disturb this wise calm, this sanity of soul; he had noticed how quickly the seamen, and Wesley in particular, had put a halt to Joe's sacrilegious rebellion—no, they wouldn't have fellows like Joe "foul everything up." And what was this "everything?" . . . it was a way of life, at sea; it meant equality, sharing, cooperation, and communal peace . . . a stern brotherhood of men, by George, where the malefactor is quickly dealt with and where the just man finds his right station. Yes, where he had once felt a deficiency of idealism in Wesley, he now found more idealism, and more practical affirmation of ideals there than in his own self.

Bill took a last look at the night sea and went below to sleep. He stretched in his bunk and smoked a last cigarette . . . he hoped he would dream.

Wesley was up before sunrise for his next watch. The bo-sun told him to do something around the deck, so Wesley picked out a broom and went around sweeping. No one was around.

The sea was rougher that second morning out, its swells less smooth and more aggravated by a wind that had picked up during the night. Wesley went topsides and watched the smoke fly from the funnel in ragged leeward shapes. He began to sweep along the deck, still dull with sleep and not able to stop yawning, until he reached aft. Two soldiers stood below him, near the four-inch gun, consorting like monsters in their earphones and orange lifebelts.

They waved at Wesley; he waved his broom.

The ship had begun to rock in the heavier swells, its stern jogging slowly in massive wobbles. The wind whipped across the waters sporting a dark green shadow of chasing ripples; here and there, a wave broke at the top and crested down a white edge of foam. In a few days, Wesley mused, rough seas would develop.

In the East now the sun had sent forth its pink heralds; a long sash laned to the ship, like a carpet of rose for Neptune. Wesley leaned on his broom and watched for the sunrise with a silent, profound curiosity. He had seen sunrise everywhere, but it never rose in the shaggy glory that it did in North Atlantic waters, where the keen, cold ocean and smarting winds convened to render the sun's young light a primitive tinge, a cold grandeur surpassed only in the further reaches of the north. He had seen wild colors off the Norwegian North Cape, but down here off the top of Maine there was more of a warm, winey splendor in the sunrise, more of a commingling of the South with the North.

Wesley walked forward and breathed the salt-seeped wind deep into his lungs. He pounded his chest joyfully and waved the broom around his head, and since no one was around, he hopped around the deck like a gleeful witch with his broom.

This was it! That air, that water, the ship's gentle plunges, the way a universe of pure wind drove off the *Westminster*'s smoke and absorbed it, the way white-capped waves flashed green, blue, and pink in the primordial dawn light, the way this Protean ocean extended its cleansing forces up, down, and in a terrific cyclorama to all directions.

Wesley stopped near the bridge and watched the destroyer up ahead. Its low form seemed to stalk the waters menacingly, her masts pitching gently from side to side, her guns alternately pointing above and below the horizons as though nothing could escape her range.

Wesley put aside the broom and sauntered around the deck. He found an oil can and went over to check the lifeboat pulleys; when he knelt down to oil one of them, the bridge house tinkled its bell. The wind whipped away the sound quickly.

"Brring, brring . . ." mimicked Wesley whimsically. "Music to my ears, damn it."

In five minutes, the sun appeared above the horizon, a rose hill rising gently to command the new day. The wind seemed to hesitate in homage.

Wesley finished his work around the deck and clambered down a ladder to the next level; he took one last deep breath of the air and pushed open a door that lead midships. When he shuffled into the galley, Glory was already up preparing breakfast.

"Mawnin'!" boomed Glory. "If you lookin' for breakfast, man, you goin' to wait!"

"Just a cup o' coffee, Pops," smiled Wesley.

Glory began to hum the blues while Wesley poured himself a cup of hot coffee.

"Where you from?" asked Wesley, jetting a stream of evaporated milk into his coffee.

"Richmond!" boomed Glory, removing his pipe. "I done lay down a hipe when I left Richmond."

Wesley stirred his coffee: "I worked on a construction job down near Richmond once."

"Richmond!" sang Glory, "dat's my town, man. I pulled outa there on account of a woman, yessuh!"

A seaman came in and unlocked the galley portholes; the pink light poured into the room with a gust of salty breeze.

Glory gazed through the porthole and shook his head slowly, like a great lion.

"I done put down a hipe when I left Richmond," he moaned deeply. "A lowdown hipe!"

"What did your woman do?" asked Wesley.

"Man, she didn't do nawthin' . . . I done it all, old Glory done it all. I lost all her money in a crap game."

Wesley shook with silent laughter. Glory poked his enormous finger in Wesley's chest: "Man, you think I was goin' to hang around there till she slit my gut?"

"No sir!"

"Hell, no! I done pull out o' Richmond an' dragged me North to New Yawk. I done worked up there for the W.P.A., in restaurants, and man, all the time, I had them lowdown woman blues." Glory chuckled with a rich growl. "I thought o' comin' on back to Richmond, but man I didn't have the guts . . . I shipped out!"

Wesley sipped his coffee silently.

"Everybody," sang Glory in his thunderous basso, "want to go to heaven . . . but no-one want to die!"

"What was her name?" Wesley asked.

Glory pushed a pan of bacon into the range oven and kicked it shut.

"Louise!" he moaned. "Louise . . . the sweetest gal I ever know." He began to sing as he broke eggs into a pot for scramble: "Lawise, Lawise, is the sweetest gal I know, hmmm, she made me walk from Chicago to the Gulf of Mexico . . . now looka here Lawise, what you tryin' to do? Hmmm? What you tryin' to do, you tryin' to give the man mah lovin'—an' me too—now, you know Lawise, baby that will never do . . . now, you know you can't love me . . . an' love some other man too . . . hmmm . . ."

His voice broke off in sinking tremolo.

"Way down blues, man," said Wesley.

"Richmond blues!" boomed Glory. "I used to sing 'Louise' all day in front o' the pool hall . . . an' den at night I done drag my feet over to Louise's. Man, you ever see Virginia in the Spring, hmmm?"

"You Goddamned right I did," said Wesley.

"Ever take yo woman out thar with a bottle o' gin, them willow trees, them nights out thar with a big fat moon jus' lookin' down, hmmm?"

"You Goddamned right I did!"

"Man, you know all 'bout it! Do I have to tell ya?" boomed Glory.

"No sir!"

"Hoo hoo hoo!" howled Glory. "I'm headin' back for Richmond soon's I drag my pants off dis ship . . . yassuh! I'm goin' on down agin!"

"I'll go with you, man! We'll spend three weeks with a couple o' them Richmond mommas!"

"Yeah!" thundered Glory. "I'm gonna get me mah honey Lawise an' you amble on down de street an' get you sump tin'."

"High yaller!" cried Wesley, slapping Glory on the back. "You an' me's goin' to have three weeks o' Richmond beach . . ."

"Hoo!" cried Glory. "Throw me dat Jelly Roll, boy, an' I'm gonna eat it right up!"

They hooted with laughter as the ship pushed on, the sun now peered into the galley port with a flaming orange face; the sea had become a great flashing blue gem specked with beads of foam.

CHAPTER EIGHT

That afternoon, while Everhart sat sunning near the poop deck rail, reading Coleridge's "Ancient Mariner," he was startled by the harsh ringing of a bell behind him.

He looked up from the book and glanced around the horizon with fear. What was it?

A droning, nasal voice spoke over the ship's address system: "All hands to the boat deck. All hands to the boat deck." The system whistled deafeningly.

Bill grinned and looked around, fear surging in his breast. The other seamen, who had been lounging on the deck with him, now dashed off. The warm wind blew Bill's pages shut; he rose to his feet with a frown and laid down the book on his folding chair. This calm, sunny afternoon at sea, flashing greens and golds, whipping bracing breezes across lazy decks, was this an afternoon for death? Was there a submarine prowling in these beautiful waters?

Bill shrugged and ran down to his focastle for the lifebelt; running down the alleyway, he hastily strapped it on, and clambered up the first ladder. An ominous silence had fallen over the ship.

"What the hell's going on!" he muttered as he climbed topsides. "This is no time for subs! We've just started!" His legs wobbled on the ladder rungs.

On the top deck, groups of quiet seamen stood beside their lifeboats, a grotesque assemblage in lifebelts, dungarees, cook's caps, aprons, oiler's caps, bow caps, khaki pants, and dozens of other motley combinations of dress. Bill hastened toward his own lifeboat and halted beside a group. No one spoke. The wind howled in the smoking funnel, flapped along the deck waving the clothing of the seamen, and rushed out over the stern along the bright green wake of the ship. The ocean sighed a soothing, sleepy hush, a sound that pervaded everywhere in suffusing enormity as the ship slithered on through, rocking gently forward.

Bill adjusted his spectacles and waited.

"Just a drill, I think," offered a seaman.

One of the Puerto Rican seamen in Bill's group, who wore a flaring cook's cap and a white apron beneath his lifebelt, began to conga across the deck while a comrade beat a conga rhythm on his thighs. They laughed.

The bell rang again; the voice returned: "Drill dismissed. Drill dismissed."

The seamen broke from groups into a confused swarm waiting to file down the ladders. Bill took off his lifebelt and dragged it behind him as he sauntered forward. Now he had seen everything . . . the ship, the sea . . . mornings, noons, and nights of sea . . . the crew, the destroyer ahead, a boat drill, everything.

He felt suddenly bored. What would he do for the next three months?

Bill went down to the engine room that night to talk with Nick Meade. He descended a steep flight of iron steps and stopped in his tracks at the sight of the monster source of the *Westminster's* power . . . great pistons charged violently, pistons so huge one could hardly expect them to move with such frightening rapidity. The *Westminster's* shaft turned enormously, leading its revolving body toward the stern through what seemed to Bill a giant cave for a giant rolling serpent.

Bill stood transfixed before this monstrous power; he began to feel annoyed. What were ideas in the face of these brutal pistons; pounding up and down with a force compounded of nature and intriguing with nature against the gentle form of man?

Bill descended further, feeling as though he were going down to the bottom of the sea itself. What chance could a man have down here if a torpedo should ram at the water-line, when the engine room deck was at a level thirty or forty feet below! Torpedo . . . another brutal concoction of man, by George! He tried to imagine a torpedo slamming into the engine room against the hysterical, blind power of the pistons, the deafening shock of the explosion, the hiss of escaping steam, the billions of water pouring in from a sea of endless water, himself lost in this holocaust and be-ing pitched about like a leaf in a whirlpool. Death! . . . he half expected it to happen that precise moment.

A water tender stood checking a gauge.

"Where's the oiler Meade?" shouted Bill above the roar of the great engine. The water tender pointed forward. Bill walked until he came to a table where Nick sat brood-ing over a book in the light of a green shaded lamp.

Nick waved his hand; he had apparently long given up conversation in an engine room, for he pushed a book to-ward Bill. Bill propped himself up on the table and ran through the leaves.

"Words, words, words," he droned, but the din of the engine drowned out his words and Nick went on reading.

The next day—another sun drowned day—the *West-minster* steamed North off the coast of Nova Scotia, about forty miles offshore, so that the crew could see the dim purple coastline just before dusk.

A fantastic sunset began to develop . . . long sashes of lavender drew themselves above the sun and reached thin shapes above distant Nova Scotia. Wesley strolled aft, digesting his supper, and was surprised to see a large congregation of seamen on the poop deck. He advanced curiously.

A man stood before the winch facing them all and speaking with gestures; on the top of the winch, he had placed a bible, and he now referred to it in a pause. Wesley recognized him as the ship's baker.

"And they were helped against them, and the Hagarites were delivered into their hand, and all that were with them," the baker shouted, "for they cried to God in the battle and he was entreated of them because they put their trust in him . . ."

Wesley glanced around at the assemblage. The seamen seemed reluctant to listen, but none of them made any motion to leave. Some watched the sunset, others the water, others gazed down—but all were listening. Everhart stood at the back listening curiously.

"And so, brothers," resumed the baker, who had obviously appointed himself the *Westminster*'s spiritual guide for the trip, "we must draw a lesson from the faith of the

Reubenites in their war with the Hagarites and in our turn call to God's aid in our danger. The Lord watched over them and he will watch over us if we pray to him and entreat his mercy in this dangerous ocean where the enemy waits to sink our ship . . ."

Wesley buttoned up his peacoat; it was decidedly chilly. Behind the baker's form, the sunset pitched alternately over and below the deck rail, a florid spectacle in pink. The sea was deep blue.

"Let us kneel and pray," shouted the baker, picking up his bible, his words drowned in a sudden gust of sea wind so that only those nearby heard him. They knelt with him. Slowly, the other seamen dropped to their knees. Wesley stood in the midst of the bowed shapes.

"Oh God," prayed the baker in a tremulous wail, "watch over and keep us in our journey, oh Lord, see that we arrive safely and . . ."

Wesley shuffled off and heard no more. He went to the bow and faced the strong headwind blowing in from the North, its cold tang biting into his face and fluttering back his scarf like a pennant.

North, in the wake of the destroyer, the sea stretched a seething field which grew darker as it merged with the lowering sky. The destroyer prowled.